Some readers' thoug

C000246853

"*A delightful read about a mur*
the viewpoint of a young libran
own experience to weave an intriguing tale."
    Richard Ashen (South Chingford Community Library)

"*I couldn't put it down! I was engaged with the characters from the very beginning.*"

"*I could not resist reading it in one go! Well-paced with action interspersed with red herrings, possible shady suspects, and some nice passages of information which, ultimately are inconsequential, but are actually very interesting. Characterisations are excellent – especially Aunt Madge! I love Aunt Madge!*"

"*An enjoyable read with a twist in who done it. I spent the entire read trying to decide what was a clue and what wasn't... Kept me thinking the entire time. I call that a success.*"

"*A delicious distraction... What a lovely way to spend an afternoon!*"

"*I really identified with Jan – the love of stories from an early age, and the careers advice – the same reaction I got – no one thought being a writer was something a working class girl did! The character descriptions are wonderfully done.*"

A MIRROR MURDER
A Jan Christopher Mystery – Book One
By Helen Hollick

Copyright © 2020 Helen Hollick
Cover Design © 2020 Cathy Helms Avalon Graphics
Set in Palatino by Pulcheria Press

ISBN 978-1-8381318-0-7 (paperback)
ISBN 978-1-8381318-1-4 (e-book)

Published by Taw River Press
https://www.tawriverpress.co.uk

eyelids and curling false eyelashes. Gloria had a boyfriend who lived nearby, although I secretly thought she could do much better for herself than Eddie Jones, a television repair man from Radio Rentals.

I glanced again at the clock. Was it moving? It didn't look like it! A young teenage girl, about fourteen, I would guess, came up to the counter to ask if we had any books on Hawaii.

"I should think so," I said, "do you want me to show you where they are?"

I passed a fruitful few minute with her. It turned out that she wanted to know more about the Pacific Islands because she was a fan of TV's *Hawaii Five-O* starring the dishy Jack Lord. Browsing through one of the information books I showed her, I discovered that the 'Five-O' represented the fact that Hawaii was the fiftieth state of America. Every so often I became restless and felt tired of working in a library, but coming across these sort of interesting 'I didn't know that' facts always won out over the bouts of monotony.

As I stamped out the two books she'd selected, I'm afraid I couldn't resist the famous quote that was said at the end of each episode: "Book 'em, Danno!"

She had the grace to laugh, which was nice of her.

Seven-forty. I heaved a few more returned books on to the trolley and looked up to see Mrs Norris leaving in a flustered hurry. How odd. She *never* left early.

"Are you all right?" I called, but I don't think she heard, because she merely muttered, "Oh dear, oh dear," as she hauled her way through the equally as obnoxious 'Out' door. I noticed that she still had the packet of biscuits in her bag, along with the entire Daily Mirror newspaper, which annoyed me a little as it had an article about one of the ex-Beatles, which I'd wanted to read all day, but hadn't found the chance. The group had split up last year, but this was something about Paul McCartney's impending new release, *Ram*. George Harrison had always been my favourite, but Paul did write some terrific songs. Briefly, I toyed with running after her, but a gentleman came up to the counter with a pile of books to be date stamped, one needing a new 'return by' date label sticking in, and then the ink ran out on the date stamp and I had to search for the other one, which I found under the deputy-head librarian's coat, which she'd lain over the end of the counter. By the time the man hoisted his books – tomes on the history of Roman Britain – into his arms, and said good night, Mrs Norris was long gone.

I filed the book tickets away in the trays, added them to the total loans for the day, and at eight o'clock, sighed with relief as Bert slammed the huge, solid wooden front doors shut and shoved the bolts home.

It was Friday evening, looked like it was about to pour with rain, and I had a twenty-five-minute walk home, or a wait, equally as long, for the bus. But tomorrow was Saturday, my one-in-three weekends off. A whole two days to myself.

Or so I thought.

2

DETECTIVE CONSTABLE WALKER

The heavens opened as Gloria and I walked out onto the paved area in front of the library with its stone walled rose beds and a wooden bench on the far side; a nice place to sit and eat a sandwich lunch on days when the sun bothered to pay us a visit. Or, in Gloria's case, to puff on a Dunhill cigarette. Gloria opened her see-through umbrella and pulled up the collar of her vinyl mac, shouted goodbye, and ran off to where Eddie was waiting in his battered Mini van with its distinctive psychedelic yellow, blue and green swirls painted across the back doors. I stood a moment, getting wet, wondering whether to walk home, or run for the bus stop. Was it worth paying a fare for such a short ride? On the other hand, the walk would be up hill, and the rain was cold, and there was a lot of it.

Then I heard my name being called. A middle-aged, smartly dressed man was getting out of a white car, beckoning me: "Jan! Jan – over here!"

Oh joy! I trotted towards him, my sandals and tights getting even more soaked from the expanding puddles.

"Uncle Toby! Am I glad to see you!" I grinned as he opened the rear door of his Jaguar and I climbed in, mindful of my soggy apparel getting the leather seat damp. I pulled a tartan blanket over from the other side, and sat on that.

My uncle settled himself in the front passenger seat and waved his hand informally at the young man sitting behind the steering wheel. "This is my new temporary Detective Constable," he said. "DC Lawrence Walker, meet my niece, Jan Christopher."

I smiled, and DC Walker turned round to smile back and hold out his hand for me to shake.

"Pleased to meet you, miss." He had a nice voice, with a slight accent, which I couldn't place.

"And you, Detective Constable, although I hope you don't end up with a broken leg, like the man you are covering for has done!"

Uncle Toby snorted laughter. "That accident was not my fault. DC Stanbridge fell off a ladder while decorating his kitchen, or that's what he said happened. Rumour has it that, actually, he tripped over his cat."

DC Walker started the engine, put the car in gear, and, indicating, looked round to ensure it was safe to move off. "Where do we take the young lady, sir?" he asked, smiling into the mirror so I could see his grey eyes shining at me.

"Oh, Jan lives with my good lady wife and myself," my uncle explained. "Has done ever since her father, my brother, passed away."

Walker's smile wavered slightly into a small frown.

Don't say it I thought. *Don't say that you've heard of my dad, DI Christopher, who was shot dead by a person or persons unknown when I was a child.*

To ensure he didn't, I said quickly, "Anyone ever told you that you look like Cary Grant?"

DC Walker laughed, "Grant in his younger years, I hope! But yes, I'm told it often. It's the cleft in my chin that does it, I think."

He drew to a halt at the traffic lights at the top of Hall Lane, indicated left, and when the lights changed, took us towards the steep hill that was known as The Mount. I turned away from the cemetery that ran to the side of the hill; both Mum and Dad were buried there. My dead sister, too, I assumed, although I was not sure of that. I looked instead at the Old Church squatting on the crest of the hill like a broody mother hen with her chicks, the houses and shops of South Chingford, scattered around her. It had a proper saint's name, but no one except the vicar called it anything but 'The Old Church'. There was a print of it in the library as it had been in the 1840s, covered in ivy and with no roof. It was restored in the 1930s, but I didn't frequent church services often, apart from Christmas and funerals. Weddings were always at the main parish church in North Chingford. Dad's funeral had been conducted at the Old Church. I was too young to attend. Too young to remember. I turned my attention back to the conversation.

"Mr Cary Grant's looks, but not his financial status, eh?" Uncle Toby laughed. He was a kind, quiet, man, born two years after Dad, in 1918. He went to Cambridge, but left in 1939 to join the police force because, for some reason which he never spoke of, he was exempt from joining up. During the war he did something that he also never talked about, beyond saying that it was, "At a place called Bletchley, and to do with maps." When the war ended, he returned to the police as a Detective Sergeant and then Detective Inspector. As of four years ago, he had become Detective Chief Inspector Christopher of Chingford Police, one rank above my dad, who had been a DI.

"Walker is new to Chingford," Uncle Toby said, "perhaps you could show him around, Jan? Help him feel at home here in our back-of-beyond London suburb?"

Awkward. Me, awkward, I mean. I was shy with young men. I'd had a couple of spotty-faced boyfriends, but there had been nothing more than a disastrous birthday party, where someone had brought a bottle of vodka, was sick all over the carpet and the parents of the hostess had then thrown us all out (to my relief, I'd hated every moment.) There had been some boring evenings at the youth club where I mostly sat on my own in a corner, while said 'boyfriend' played table tennis or Subbuteo, both of which I was hopeless at, and all followed with a few embarrassing kisses. I had cried buckets when boyfriend Roland had gone off on the organised school trip to Russia in February 1969 – a joint effort between the boys' and girls' sides of the school in preparation for the mixed-sex amalgamation the following year. I knew that Roly would find a new girlfriend while he was away. He did. The rat. (Ironic that several years later TV had a puppet called Roland Rat. I always imagined who it was named after.)

But, "I'd like that," DC Walker said. "Maybe we could borrow your car, sir?"

"Don't push your luck," Uncle replied, with a pretence of sternness. Walker grinned at me via the mirror. He'd already worked out that the Jag was my Uncle's pride and joy, and that a mere DC only drove it when on duty.

"There's not much to see or do around here," I stated. "Some historic sights, a few mediocre shops, and that's about it."

"There are several decent restaurants," Uncle objected.

It had stopped raining as DC Walker parked up in the drive outside the house, a four-bedroom detached property in the posh part of The Ridgeway. He got out and opened the door for me. I liked him. He was sweet, although I wasn't quite sure if 'sweet' suited a Detective Constable. Perhaps there was a rougher, tougher, side to him when it came to chasing dangerous criminals?

"A meal would be nice. Canteen food is a little, um, bland," DC Walker said, then added, "if you wouldn't object to me taking your niece out for a meal, that is, sir?"

"Not at all, as long as you bring her safe home again. But I'm not sure that 'bland' is the right description? 'Awful' would probably be more appropriate?"

I knew what Uncle Toby was up to, the cunning so-and-so. I rarely went out because I had no one to go out with, and I partly suspected that no one asked me out because of who my uncle was. He very probably suspected the same. Who in his right mind would want to date a plain-looking, uninteresting girl, whose uncle was a Detective Chief Inspector? Who, except another, desperate for company, detective police officer?

"Tomorrow evening? Seven o'clock?" DC Walker suggested, as he opened the garage doors and wheeled out a pushbike.

"All right," I answered. I couldn't say anything else, really, could I?

He nodded, said goodnight and, head down, pedalled off.

"Does he live far away?" I asked as he disappeared round the bend in the road.

"Temporary digs at the section house, I believe," Uncle said, fishing in his pocket for the front door key. "Food as bad as our canteen, I expect."

I didn't like to admit that I had no idea where the police section house accommodation was. "It seems a bit unfair," I observed, "that he drives your nice car all day, but then has to go home, in the rain, on a bike."

Uncle chuckled, "Never fear, sweetheart, the exercise will do him good."

Aunt Madge was in the kitchen, the smell of chicken with lemon sauce, deliciously tempting. She popped her head round the corner, blew a kiss to us both, and seeing my rain-bedraggled appearance, suggested I run upstairs to put something dry on before I caught my death. I heard her thank Uncle Toby for picking me up, and the smack of a resounding kiss. Whether it was her kissing him, or him her, I didn't know. Nor was it any of my business. They had been married for many years, and were as much in love as they had been on their wedding day.

INTERLUDE: DC LAURIE WALKER

I realised that I might have made a mistake in transferring from Devon to London 'for experience' on the day I arrived in Hackney. The smell was the first thing I noticed: petrol fumes, rotting detritus in the streets; the East End London suburb stank. The second thing was the noise. Cars, lorries, buses; people. But I needed the experience if I was going to make an even half-decent CID detective, a Detective Sergeant at least, although I had my sight set on Inspector. Happy dreams, Laurie lad! London, I can tell you, is most definitely *not* North Devon!

I had been based in Barnstaple, a Georgian town on the banks of the River Taw, (which is where Henry Williamson set his famous novel, *Tarka The Otter* – not many otters around now, alas.) I say 'Georgian'; the Saxons were there back in 1066, probably the Romans before them, but the 'boom' came when the tobacco and sugar trade from the American Colonies took off in the 1700s. My folks live upriver from Barnstaple, in a village six miles from the smaller town of South Molton, which is not far from Exmoor. Now, if you like and want remote, then Exmoor is your place, although Dartmoor, in the same county but down to the south, is even more isolated. That's one of the reasons they built a prison there.

I missed the quiet of Devon, the expanse of the stars on a dark night – no street lights in most of the villages. The kind people, the quiet accent. Devon is on a different timeline, I think, we do everything at half-pace down there. Not for Devonians the rush and bustle of snappy, get it done yesterday, London. Things in Devon are done 'dreckly', which is code for 'soon', although when 'soon' might be, is anyone's guess. Within the month. If you're lucky. And there's less crime in Devon. Much less crime. It comes to something when the major incident of the week is that someone has stolen the notice board from outside a village hall. (I'm not joking!) Which is why I transferred to London. Like I said, for the experience.

Several weeks in, and I wished I hadn't. It wasn't just the dirt and the stench, my main discomfort was the obnoxious people: foul mouthed, arrogant, ignorant bullies. And no, I don't mean the criminals, the vice gangs, thieves, murderers and pimps. I mean the men who were my fellow police officers. Not all of them, there were a few good guys, but too many were out for what they could get for themselves. Frankly, I would rather deal with a nest of adult, glare-eyed, pink-tailed, flea-riddled brown rats, than spend too many months at the station I was assigned to. Corruption and violence were rife. Need a confession? Then beat it out of a likely suspect, especially if he was black: any black man, or even black woman, would do. I found that disgusting. Whatever happened to 'equal rights for all'?

I wasn't liked. Understandable, I was from the sticks, the very distant sticks at that. And I was only a green-behind-the-ears DC, but I had hopes, dreams and standards. I loathed their use of the disgraceful 'N' word, their unnecessary swearing, their lack of respect for foreigners and women. Politeness and courtesy cost nothing, but can reap great reward. My way of doing things was by the book, following the letter of the law, because if the law-keepers break the law then what hope is there for order and justice? Among these men, the arm of the law was long enough to reach into the deepest cesspit and *still* come up smelling of fake roses.

The personal bullying I could handle, I'd not make a very good copper if some spiteful name-calling upset me, would I? Although the mocking of my slight accent did irritate. I don't have the typical West Country yawl; the 'arr' made famous by Robert Newton's performance as Long John Silver in *Treasure Island*, because my folks come from Buckinghamshire. They moved to Devon when I was seven, so my accent was Home Counties, but I had picked up a few Devonian traits, 'f' was a 'v' sound, so 'vamly' for family, 'vine' for fine – 'vor' for for! Teasing I didn't mind, but some of my colleagues were outright nasty, and I'm talking senior officers here, not mere on-the-beat constables.

One constable was a friend, Tom Rogers. He had the cubbyhole next to me at the section house, (I can't describe it as a room, that would be too grand a description.) He was a friend because he was a Brummie. His Birmingham accent was mocked more than my Devonshire one. The difference between us: he didn't mind. I did.

Which was partly, no I lie, *totally*, why I jumped at the chance when word came through that a temporary Detective Constable was required for Chingford Police. The grumbling about the request was immense. Chingford was the outpost of nowhere, the countryside, where nothing happened. There were few 'tarts', and even fewer pubs, they all grumbled. No one wanted to go, so I was 'volunteered'.

"The local yokels want a DC," I was told by the superintendent. "We haven't one to spare, so you wouldn't mind filling in for a couple of months, would you, Walker? Good lad, I knew I could rely on you!"

Had they asked nicely I would have said yes like a shot, but even shoehorned in, I was not going to quibble about their crude methods. I was told to go, so I went. Happily.

Best thing I've ever done, I reckon. I liked DCI Christopher right from the start. He was welcoming, respectful and expected me to do my job to the best of my ability, as, equally, he expected to do his. He took his job seriously. The rest of the men at Chingford Station seemed decent as well, possibly because of Tobias Christopher's influence. No one on his watch messed about – in the break-the-rules department, I mean. In the laughter category there was plenty of it abounding in a friendly, camaraderie atmosphere. And because of it, the work got done with a will and a sense of pride.

For my own pride, I was honoured on my second day to be given the keys to the DCI's Jaguar, along with the post of officially becoming his bagman and driver. It was his injured DC I was replacing, so I was automatically slotted in to the role, but I think I would have been chained to a desk if Christopher hadn't, reciprocally, taken a liking to, and trusted, me. I was well aware that I had to ensure I lived up to that liking and trust.

The first week was routine stuff: a break-in to a kiddies' clothing shop, a minor attempted arson on a garden shed. Three burglaries. Several tons of paperwork. I spent an entire afternoon studying a local map, familiarising myself with the area, the roads, where the pubs were located – where any toms (prostitutes) hung out. (For any of you who are wondering – the railway station car park and a couple of the less salubrious public houses.)

On the Friday, we looked into what seemed to be an organised effort at stealing petrol from cars parked at the railway station, which, through a tip-off, led us to questioning the landlord of one of the pubs in South Chingford. He was lying through his teeth about the stolen petrol, but with nothing concrete to go on, there was not much more we could do. For now.

The day had been overcast, sombre and grey, and by

evening, although it was July, the rain had set in bringing dusk on early.

DCI Christopher – by now I had discovered that no one called him 'Tobias', he was 'Toby' or 'Sir' – suggested that, as we were passing, we could pick up his niece from her place of work. I had no objection, especially when she climbed into the car and the DCI introduced her.

"This is my new temporary Detective Constable," he said to her. "DC Lawrence Walker, meet my niece, Jan Christopher."

I did not believe in love at first sight, but when she smiled at me?

Well, I do now.

4

A FOREST ENCOUNTER

Saturday morning dawned bright and fresh, not that I was awake early enough to see, or even hear, the arrival of dawn heralded, so I believe, by the numerous birds in the back garden. I was up for breakfast, though, enticed from my bed by the wafting smell of frying bacon. Only Aunt Madge was in the kitchen. On the table, an empty plate and cutlery smeared with the remnants of toast, bacon and eggs.

"Uncle Toby already gone?" I asked as I sat down to a 'Full English' of sausages, bacon, scrambled egg, fried bread and tomatoes, which my beloved aunt placed with a flourish before me.

"He has," she confirmed. "The new DC was here on the dot of eight o'clock. He seems a nice young man. Polite. Tea or coffee?"

"Tea, please." I made no mention of the 'nice young man', but Aunt Madge could be most persistent when she got the bit between her teeth.

"I hear he is taking you out for a meal?"

"Yes, I think Uncle Toby is concerned that he might be lonely."

"Are you coming riding with me this morning?" she asked

a few minutes later as she poured tea for us both from the blue and white china teapot.

I glanced out of the kitchen window, noticed Basil, my aunt's notorious black cat disappearing over the garden fence, no doubt intent on undertaking his *toilette* in next door's vegetable patch.

"Yes, please," I grinned. The sky was blue, the sun was shining. I had nothing else to do on my day off. As if I would say anything else – even had it been raining as much as last night. I loved horse riding, and Aunt Madge's two horses were a joy to hack through the six-thousand acres or so of London's Epping Forest. Not that we could ride over all of it! For most of the busier parts of the forest, horse riders had to remain on the designated tracks and bridle paths, but that still gave us plenty of scope to enjoy ourselves.

We had ridden for about an hour, hacking over towards High Beach, where we dismounted and stopped at the tea hut for a cuppa and a lump of homemade fruit cake each – most of which we shared with the two horses, Rajah and Kaler. Being a sunny Saturday, the little car park was almost full with families enjoying a weekend day out, and, inevitably, there were several motorbikes with their leather-clad bikers hanging around. They scared me, especially the youths with their tattoos and air of rough bravado.

"They are only lads out for a good time," Madge said, noticing my unease. "It's the newspapers that have given them such a bad name. Most of the 1960s enmity between the Mods and Rockers has fizzled out, but the press likes to stir up public concern. There was a headline in one of the red tops the other day, blazing the words, 'Rocker Rave-Up Rant' and giving the impression of a free-for-all fight, but the article went on to say there was no violence! Toby says the papers, with their irresponsible exaggerating, do more damage and harm than any biker group."

I knew what she said was true, but I didn't feel very reassured, so I kept Rajah between me and the youths while we enjoyed our snack.

After dropping our empty polystyrene cups into the waste bin, Aunt Madge swung up into Kaler's saddle, not at all flustered by the fact that her bay thoroughbred was snorting and prancing about, pretending to be frightened of a couple struggling to wheel a toddler strapped into a Maclaren pushchair over the stony ground. The baby was enjoying itself; mum, doing the hard work of pushing, wasn't. Rajah, a silver dun Connemara, and the smaller of the two horses by four inches at fifteen-two hands high, was ignoring the pushchair, intent on eyeing up a nearby child who was waving a dripping ice cream cornet around. He loved the wafer bit and had been known to snatch the treat from unsuspecting children – much like seagulls steal chips at the seaside. I hauled his head around and mounted, although not as elegantly as Madge had. My face then burned bright red when one of the bikers called out, "I'd enjoy 'er mountin' me like that!"

Partly, my red face was because, in my eighteen-year-old extreme naivety, I didn't fully understand what he meant, but guessed, by the ensuing laughter, that it was something crude.

Madge nudged Kaler sideways – he looked quite impressive when he was showing off and prancing about, head up, neck and tail arched, nostrils snorting, feet dancing. Using her heel, she moved him nearer the bikers, who instantly scattered as he jigged too close.

"Goodness, boys," Madge said, perfectly seriously, "it's only a horse! And I'm afraid you're nowhere near *big* enough to appreciate grown-up activities." She laughed, winked at me and kicked Kaler into a canter straight from a standstill. I followed her, at a more sedate trot, and as soon as we turned onto the bridle path, we gave the horses their heads into a glorious gallop, aiming back towards Bury

Woods and the livery yard where Madge kept her equine darlings.

The horses were sweating as we eased to a trot, then a walk, and I confess, I was breathless as well. I could never understand how Madge could keep her hair, make-up and poise so pristine even while out riding. I guess it was because she came from a well-to-do family, and had gone to a finishing school for young ladies before she met my uncle at a policemen's ball soon after the war, and fallen in love.

We let the horses amble up the last sandy ride, enjoying the dappled sunlight filtering through the oaks, hornbeams, birch and beech trees. Madge brought a packet of cigarettes and her American Zippo from her jacket pocket, and lit up, blowing a stream of blue-white smoke into the air in pleasurable satisfaction. She never smoked indoors at home, nor in the stable yard, but would often nip up to the back garden shed for a surreptitious puff after dinner each evening. I suspected that she smoked a lot more when she was out shopping or visiting friends, but did not think it my place to pry. Uncle Toby used to smoke a pipe when I was little, I remembered watching him pack the bowl with tobacco and puff away as he lit it. I liked the smell of the smoke, but he gave up soon after I came to live with them, after Dad had died and Mum... Well, I never thought of Mum. She disappeared from my life one day, a few weeks after Dad had been shot dead. I admit, I didn't miss her. We didn't get on. I don't know if that would have changed as I grew older, but I suspect not. I don't remember her as cruel or unkind, but nor do I remember her as loving. In truth, I only remember her at all from the two photographs that Uncle had of her and Dad on their wedding day, and my sister June and me on her lap when we were tiny babies.

Without warning, Kaler stopped dead, his feet planted foursquare, head up, ears flicking, staring intently into the overgrown woodland to the left ahead of us. Rajah stopped, too. Madge and I peered into the thicket of leaves, but could see, or hear, nothing.

"Probably only a squirrel," Madge said, giving Kaler a nudge with her heel – but all four of us jumped when a man crashed out from one of the bushes, wearing a grey rain mac held open wide, a Micky Mouse mask covering his face – and absolutely *nothing* else. I had never, ever, seen a naked man. Not a real one. Paintings and statues of beautiful young, athletic men did not look one bit like this rather inelegant, slightly chubby male standing in front of us with his 'things' on display. Michelangelo's *David* he was most certainly not!

Madge took a puff of her cigarette, and again asked Kaler to walk on. The surprise over, he did so, sidling around the man by curving his sleek body away as if the flasher was a poisonous snake.

I kept Rajah firmly on the other side of Madge, and several yards further on she said, very loudly, "For the life of me, if that small apology of a willy was all I had to show, I'd keep it very well hidden!"

Bright red, I glanced back over my shoulder. The man had disappeared, but I felt uneasy, the unease intensifying as we turned the horses onto the road and passed several parked cars.

"We had better telephone Toby from the tack room payphone when we get back to the yard," Madge said, "and put in a report. Although by the time anyone gets here, that imbecile would have long gone."

I said nothing. He'd had brown, curly hair poking out from beneath that mask, and I thought I had caught a glimpse of a tattoo on the side of his neck: a bird, I thought. Blue ink against white skin. One of the parked cars was a Mini van with psychedelic back doors. I recognised it without doubt. It belonged to Gloria's boyfriend, Eddie Jones. He had brown, curly hair, a bird tattoo on his neck and was prancing around in the woods, naked except for a mac and a mask.

5

A NIGHT OUT

The telephone rang at five-thirty shortly after Uncle Toby had
got home. Aunt Madge answered it. I heard her voice from
my bedroom upstairs, where I was bashing out the words, on
my battered old typewriter, of another chapter for my
potential best seller science fiction novel.

"Hello? 5785." A pause. "Jan! It's for you, dear."

I ran down the stairs and took the receiver from her,
waited a moment while she wandered back into the kitchen –
obviously listening. I heard her whisper something to Uncle
Toby. Not for the first time, or last, I wished we had more
than one telephone in the house, or that this one wasn't in
such a very public place in the hall. If I wanted to talk
privately (which I'd never had any reason to), I would have to
use the public telephone box outside the telephone exchange
down the road.

"Hello?" I said tentatively. I rarely received phone calls,
not having many friends with any need to contact me. My
heart sank to my pink, furry, mule slippers as I heard DC
Walker's voice. This was it; he had changed his mind. Was
phoning to say our evening out was off.

"Hello, Jan." His voice sounded cheerful. Maybe...? I held
my breath. "I'm running a little late, pick you up at seven-

fifteen? I thought perhaps we could go to the pictures instead of a restaurant? They're re-running a Clint Eastwood. Would that be OK?"

Two things ran through my mind. How was he going to pick me up with a pushbike, and was he serious? Clint Eastwood? The heartthrob of the entire world? And that included my world, as small as it was. I'd adored Clint ever since his days as Rowdy Yates in *Rawhide*.

"That'll be fine, what film is it?" I asked, hoping the glow of my excitement didn't transmit into my voice, or if it did, that DC Walker didn't realise that it was directed at the thought of spending several hours with Clint Eastwood, rather than appreciating an evening out with him.

"Great. It's *Kelly's Heroes*. See you later, alligator." And he hung up.

Clint Eastwood *and* Donald Sutherland. It was my lucky day. Just by chance – as if – Aunt Madge wandered out into the hall. "Oh, was that Lawrence? He seems a nice young man."

I nodded, smiled. "We're going to the pictures. A Clint Eastwood is on at the Odeon."

I spent the intervening time checking and re-checking my hair and make-up, and changed my earrings, deciding that the long dangly ones were *too* long and dangly. I opted for my rather lovely petite rose quartz and silver teardrop earrings instead, which were more appropriate as rose quartz was supposed to be lucky for 'matters of the heart'. Maybe it was too soon to be thinking about love and Lawrence but... well, can it ever be too soon if you feel you really like someone?

I was relieved to discover that he had a car. An old, but lovingly cared for, green Morris Minor. Stupidly, I nearly burst into tears when I saw it. I had a vivid memory of a green Morris Minor. One that terrified me the older I got, as the consequences of what might have happened lingered and multiplied with each year that I grew older. Uncle Toby had saved my life, or at least saved me from serious injury. He had been – always was, come to that – my hero.

I was six years old. We lived in a different house back then, one at the top of a steep, but quiet side street. The main road ran along the bottom, and in the distance, the reservoirs that gave Londoners their water gleamed in the hot summer sunshine. We, Uncle Toby, Aunt Madge and I, were going somewhere special, I've no idea where, a function of some sort, for Uncle Toby was upstairs dressing in his best suit. I was alone, already in the back of the car trying to play a tune on a cheap plastic recorder – very badly. I suspect that was why I had been put in the car, to mute the dreadful noise a little. And then the car started moving. Faster and faster, rolling down the hill. I screamed. I leant out of the open window and banged and banged and banged that recorder on the side of the car as I screamed and screamed.

I don't remember seeing him, but my uncle told me, several years later, that he had hurtled down the stairs, leapt over the garden gate and sprinted down the hill towards the car that was rapidly gaining speed. All the windows were open, I was still screaming and banging, banging and screaming. Uncle jumped onto the running board, leant in through the passenger door window, grabbed the steering wheel and guided the car into the kerb, where it bumped up onto the grass and stopped. I have no memory of what happened next, whether we went to whatever the posh function was or not. All I knew was that my uncle had sprained his ankle badly and that, had he not stopped the car, it could have careered right into the busy main road at the bottom of the hill. (And I would not be sitting here, writing this.)

"You all right?" DC Walker's concerned voice brought me back to the present.

I smiled, composed myself. "Yes, I'm fine. Where did the car come from?"

He grinned, "It's mine, but I had a puncture, so had to

borrow a mate's bike this morning. That's why I am a little late." He kicked one of the wheels with what was obviously an air of affection. "I had to change the old girl's tyre. She's called Greenleaf, by the way."

"Now that's imaginative!" I laughed as he held the passenger door open and helped me in.

We drove off, me sitting prim with my knees neatly close together, wishing that perhaps I should not have chosen quite such a short mini-skirt, and hoping that we would not be walking far, as the shoes I'd put on were already pinching my toes.

"The film starts at just gone eight," he said changing gear as we drove down The Mount. "Do you want something to eat first? I'm sorry, I promised you a meal. Although, my fault, we haven't much time if we want the cinema as well."

I pointed to the first row of shops at the bottom of the hill. "There's fish and chips," I said, "if you don't mind eating out of the paper, we could always have that."

He grinned at me. "Good thinking, Batman."

I laughed. "Ker-pow!"

We parked a short way from the cinema and sat in the car eating cod and chips with our fingers, and drinking a bottle of Coca Cola each. And chatted. He told me that he had transferred to North London to further his career, that he'd been 'up here in Hackney' for a short while, and had been asked to transfer to Chingford to assist DCI Christopher.

"So, 'up here' from where?" I asked, licking salt and vinegar from my fingers.

"Devon, the West Country. My parents live not far from Barnstaple, I was in the 'force there."

I knew where Devon was. Had never heard of Barnstaple. I made a mental note to look it up in one of the travel guides on Monday when I got back to work.

"I'm hoping to be promoted to Detective Sergeant soon. If I do well enough here, maybe? I'm honoured to be working with your uncle. He has a good reputation for being a fair man who gets things done."

"Who catches criminals?" I laughed.

"Yes!"

"And who..." I hesitated. Dare I say this? I took a breath. "And who, some time during the day, dropped a heavy hint that I rather like Clint Eastwood?"

He laughed again. He had a nice laugh, sort of growly but homely. "Yes, to that, too. Although, he did not have to twist my arm. I like Eastwood as well."

I was pleased when we walked to the cinema as I was in rather desperate need of the Ladies – all that Coca Cola. On reappearing, I was presented with a large paper bag of popcorn, and a slab of Cadbury's Dairy Milk chocolate.

"You shouldn't have!" I said. "You bought the chips, this ought to be my treat, Lawrence." I blushed. It had been the first time I had used his name.

"Laurie, please," he answered, "Only Mum and Gran call me Lawrence. I hate it."

He showed our tickets to the usherette, and we took our seats. Only a few minutes until the curtain went up.

"What's Jan short for?" he asked, taking a handful of the popcorn. "Janet? Janice?"

"January," I reluctantly admitted, and rolled my eyes at the question leaping from his puzzled brows and forming on his lips. "Don't ask! And no one I like calls me anything but Jan."

Fortunately, the lights dimmed, and we were too engrossed in an exciting, if factually challenging, gold heist in France at the end of World War II, to talk any more.

6

A TRAGIC DISCOVERY

We were laughing as we strolled, arm in arm, back along Appletree Road to where we had left the car. I'd known Laurie for no more than twenty-four hours, but he was so easy-going, I felt like we'd been best friends forever. A woman came past us pushing a pram that had a squeaky front wheel, *whee, whee, whee,* it went.

I thought it rather late to be out with a baby. She must have read my thoughts, or correctly interpreted my disapproving expression, for she gave a half-hearted smile and explained.

"I'm out of S.M.A. M'other half is at work. I'm poppin' round to the corner shop. Couldn't leave 'er, on 'er own, could I?"

The woman looked tired, harassed, her face was red, her hair, beneath her scarf, untidy. Had I been on my own, I would have offered to go to the shop for her, except I would never have been out on my own at gone eleven at night.

There was a slight obnoxious whiff coming from the pram, but as the baby was asleep, its mother obviously didn't want to wake her to change a dirty nappy.

"S.M.A.?" Laurie asked as we walked on.

"Powdered milk for babies," I explained. "You didn't know that?"

He laughed. "I'm a detective, not a midwife."

I had my arm through his, and snuggled closer as we walked. Laurie whistled a few bars of the theme tune from the film; I joined in, humming. It had been a good film, funny in places, especially when a Sherman tank had come out from a railway tunnel blaring music, and an outdoor privy had been blown up.

A man walked past us with his Labrador dog, taking a last walk before bed, I guessed. I waited until he had gone on a good way, then giggled.

"Woof! Woof! That's my other dog impersonation!" A quote from Sutherland's mad-as-a-hatter character, Oddball.

No one else was around. I could hear water, an ornamental fountain in the front garden of number forty-four. I always found fountains to be a restful, relaxing sound, but I wondered if the immediate neighbours shared the same thought. The constant gush could be quite annoying in the middle of the night when everything else was quiet.

Laurie had laughed at my mimicry from the film. He stopped in the shadows between two of the streetlights and pulled me towards him. "The moonlight glinting on your hair," he whispered, "is quite lovely."

"There isn't a moon," I teased, making light of his words in order to fend off my face turning beetroot red. I peered up into the sky. Very few stars, only the brightest ones twinkling through the glare of the street lighting.

"I'm using my imagination," Laurie retorted. "The streetlight is a stand-in." He laughed again, and pointed at the front garden behind us. "We do have the romance of the *Fontana di Trevi*, the most famous fountain in the world, and the largest Baroque example in Rome."

I was impressed by his Italian pronunciation. "Have you seen it?" I asked.

He nodded. "I have. And the Colosseum. They'd run out

of lions, though, so I was quite safe." He started to hum *Three Coins In The Fountain*, then sang a few words: "Three coins in the fountain, each one thrown by hopeful lovers, which one will the fountain bless?" before chuckling again. "I can't sing, sorry."

"Well you can't be Cary Grant *and* Frank Sinatra! He sang that, you know, but wasn't credited for it."

"Really? I wouldn't credit that!"

It took me a moment to cotton-on to his pun. I swiped at his shoulder. "Oh, you..." but he caught my wrist, swapped to lightly holding my hand and then kissed me, a butterfly touch on my lips.

I was taken aback. I'd only known him a short while. This was a bit forward, wasn't it? I must have made some sound, for he pulled back, went red and apologised.

"Goodness, I'm so sorry. I don't know what came over me. I..."

"No," I said, "no, it's all right, it was nice." I was about to say, 'Please, do it again,' but said instead, "Look... look..." I took a few steps away from him, pointing to a mid-terrace house on the other side of the road with its front door wide open, light spilling out from the hallway beyond.

"That's Mrs Norris's house," I said, my voice starting to tremble. "Betty Norris, an elderly lady. She comes into the library every evening. Why is her door wide open at this time of night?"

Laurie frowned. We crossed the road and opening the front garden gate, walked up the overgrown garden path, my hand in his as I followed close behind.

"Norris, you say?" he asked, looking over his shoulder at me.

I nodded.

"Mrs Norris?" he called as he stepped over the threshold. "Are you in? Are you all right?"

"Betty?" I also called out. "It's me, Jan, from the library. Do you need any help?"

Laurie went into the hall and stood beside the staircase to peer upward into the shadows of the unlit landing. "Mrs Norris?" he called again, louder.

Opposite the stairs, near the front door, was a wooden combination of a coat rack and telephone table, with no telephone on it. Mrs Norris's string shopping bag lay on the tabletop, with the biscuits still in it but no newspaper. Hanging on the hooks, her coat and the pink beret. The house was silent. Eerily still.

Laurie walked further into the hall, stopped, turned to me. "You wait here, I'll investigate."

"No," I said, "you might frighten her. She knows me; I'll come with you."

We peered into the front room, Laurie feeling along the wall, just inside the open door, to find the light switch. He flicked it on. The room was very clean and tidy, but old-fashioned – very 1950s. A bay window cradled a three-seater settee with a couple of floral cushions and a pile of folded blankets set on it. Lace antimacassars were on the arms and head rest, the same on two matching armchairs set against the opposite wall. In the alcove next to the chimney breast, a round table with a wireless on it. No television set. I noticed a fluffy, blue woolly ball beneath the table. A cat's toy?

Set along the tiled mantlepiece above the bare grate of a coal fire, a clock that ticked slowly, quietly and solemnly, and three black-and-white wedding photographs in wooden frames. All were different, but the young women in each had similar features. One wore an Edwardian, early 1920s style dress, while the proud Charlie Chaplin-moustached man next to her was resplendent in a pristine army uniform. A First World War wedding, a young Mrs Norris and her bridegroom, both of them looking so happy.

The other two brides – granddaughters? – wore typical 1960s dresses, with beehive, heavily lacquered hairstyles, while one of the men had a Beatle-length haircut. Next to the photographs, a birthday card with pink roses, and the words, 'Happy Birthday Gran.'

In the next, back, room, a walnut dining table with six matching upright chairs tucked neatly beneath. Against one wall a sideboard, with above it, the closed double doors of a serving hatch. Windows and a half-glass door gave view to the night and what was, presumably, the back garden. A neat and tidy room, kept clean, but cold and deserted. A room that had not been used as a family room for years, by the look of it.

Laurie switched the light off and we went on down the hall. I could feel my heart thumping. The house was obviously looked after, for it was tidy and there was no dust or accumulation of cobwebs, but everything was old. The hall carpet matched the one on the stairs, a narrow, brown and cream runner, with a few noticeable stains on it, but the linoleum beneath had recently been mopped, for it retained a distinct lavender aroma of Flash floor cleaner. Ahead, another closed door, leading to the kitchen. Laurie pressed the door handle down, the door opened. The light was on.

"Mrs Norris? Are you here, ma'am?" Laurie called as he pushed the door open wider.

I peered in, over his shoulder.

And screamed.

Mrs Norris was lying face down on the black-and-white lino tiled floor. Blood had spread into a grotesque, wide pool beneath her head. Shards of glass and splintered wood were scattered around, the remains of a fancy wall mirror, shattered to pieces as it had smashed into her skull. A disgusting smell tainted the air.

There was no doubt. Mrs Betty Norris, the old lady who cut the food coupons from the Daily Mirror was quite dead. Had been brutally murdered.

7

ALONE IN THE KITCHEN

Laurie wanted me to sit in the car while he ran to the police telephone box situated beyond the cinema, on the island crescent where the buses terminated. I had refused.

"I can't leave her on her own!" Tears were starting to prick my eyes, and I was shaking. He was right, the car would be a better place, but despite the obnoxious odour I couldn't, just couldn't, leave Mrs Norris lying on her kitchen floor with no one to – to, what? Comfort her? Protect her? She was beyond both, but I could not bear the thought of leaving her.

I think Laurie understood, because he took his jacket off and draped it around my shoulders, sat me in one of the wooden chairs next to the kitchen table and told me, firmly, to, "Stay there. Don't move. Don't touch *anything.*"

When I looked up at him, my face half-crumpled into grief, half into bewilderment. He kissed my forehead and said, "It's a murder scene, love. The entire place will soon be crawling with coppers and SOCO – Scene of Crime Officers – looking for evidence of who did this."

I nodded. I knew that, but until he'd said it, it hadn't registered properly. "I know what SOCO means. My uncle is a Detective Chief Inspector," I said unnecessarily tartly. I immediately apologised. "I'm sorry, that was very rude of me. I'll stay put," I promised.

"No need to apologise, you're in shock." He didn't kiss me again, but he touched my cheek with a forefinger. "I won't be long." And he was gone.

I heard vomiting outside the open front door, partially rose as I guessed it was Laurie spewing his insides up, but thought better of going out to him. One: he had told me to stay put. Two: he would be embarrassed. Three: I would be embarrassed.

I was shaking again. I clutched my arms around myself and rocked back and forth, a sound between a groan and a sob leaving my throat, awful memories returning. It was not the first time for me. I'd seen my dad, my own dad, shot dead with three bullets right before my eyes. I'd been upstairs in bed, had heard someone knock, loud and insistent at the front door. Heard Dad answer it, exclaim, 'What the...?" and then scuffling and shouting.

I had run from my bedroom and peered through the spindles of the banisters. There had been three very loud bangs, and Dad had staggered backwards clutching at his chest, knocking over the telephone table with the vase of fresh flowers on it, sending it crashing to the floor. Daffodils. Bright yellow daffodils that I had helped Mum pick from the garden that afternoon. The telephone itself tinkled as it, too, fell, the Bakelite casing cracking as it smashed on to the floor. Dad tried to grab the post of the banisters as he toppled onto the bottom two stairs. There was blood everywhere, all over him, on the carpet, up the walls, red splatters and dribbles spoiling the new floral wallpaper. The only other thing I remember of that night was screaming. I stood at the top of the stairs, and I screamed, and screamed, and screamed. I had been five years old.

I felt a scream crawling up from my stomach into my mouth now, but gulped it down and clutched Laurie's jacket tighter around my shoulders. I swallowed, hard, again, suddenly desperately wanting the loo. I crossed my legs and squeezed my thighs together.

"Think of something else!" I murmured aloud.

I looked at the space where the mirror had been, a distinctive lighter patch against the cream-painted wall. The mirror must have been ripped off in anger, or frustration, for the nail, hook or screw – whatever it had been hanging on – had been yanked out of the wall, leaving the plaster cracked around a large hole. I looked again at poor Mrs Norris. She was facing away from where the mirror had been, had she turned from someone, not expecting such a vicious attack? Had there been an argument? Had she known the person who had killed her?

Unlike the dining room, and the front room, come to that, this kitchen looked lived in, bright and homely. There was nothing modern, most of the furniture and fittings reflecting the fifties: a cream-painted wall cabinet, and matching cupboard and drawers. A stove with a red kettle on one of the gas rings, its conical whistle in place. Corner shelves with three cream-coloured tins with green lids, labelled *tea, coffee, sugar.* A square, white metal bread bin. Pale blue chequered curtains, drawn across a window above the sink, with blue and white china on the draining board washed up and left to dry. A matching chequered curtain on a wire rod beneath the sink. The table I was sitting at had a blue Formica top and was pushed against the wall, the flap on that side folded down. Above, the doors of the serving hatch into the dining room. Apart from the washing up, and the blood on the floor, all was clean and tidy.

I felt beneath the striped, knitted tea cosy that covered a teapot sitting on its wooden stand on the table. Cold. Then I remembered that Laurie had told me not to touch anything. I sat back in the chair and folded my arms. It didn't seem right that Mrs Norris was lying there, abandoned. Maybe I could cover her with something? I started to get to my feet, sighed, sat down again. Laurie would be back soon; he would take care of her dignity. Then I noticed something. I bent as far forward as I could without leaving the chair, to peer closer. Something was clutched in her hand. A piece of paper, the corner of the front page of the Daily Mirror poking through her clenched fingers. I could see its distinctive white lettering on a red background. Footsteps coming down the hall! I gasped, sprang to my feet. What if the murderer had come back? Felt stupid as I heard Laurie call out.

"Only me!"

He walked in through the door, and I ran to him with a gulped sob, throwing myself into his arms. I buried my head into his home-knitted, woollen cardigan and cried. For Mrs Norris, for me, for the memory of my dad? I don't know, all I knew was that with Laurie's arms round me, holding me tight, I felt safe.

8

INTERLUDE: DC LAURIE WALKER

I had seen dead people. I'd been a copper for several years, first as a uniformed constable, then, when I passed my examinations, promotion to a Detective Constable. Policemen see all sorts of horrors, deliberate violence inflicted by cruel people, and dreadful injuries when we investigate car crashes and accidents. A tractor toppling over, I can tell you, can make a mess of a person. I had attended two murders in Devon, but for both there had been no blood. One was death by poison, the other had been a hanging made to look like suicide.

Seeing that elderly lady lying on the floor with her head bashed in, I'm ashamed to say, I reacted very unprofessionally. Doubly ashamed to admit that I heaved my guts up while Miss Christopher, Jan, seemed as cool as a cucumber. Although I did manage to hold everything together in her presence.

I tried to urge her to sit in my car which was parked a few doors down, but she was adamant that she wanted to stay with poor Mrs Norris. I admired that. That was courageous and compassionate. If that had been my gran, I would not have wanted her to be left alone lying dead on the kitchen floor. A rare pang of homesickness filled me as I recalled our

possibly instantaneous. It's likely that she would have been immediately unconscious, so even if you *had* found her alive, you wouldn't have been able to save her. It wasn't *just* the mirror that shattered." He didn't elaborate.

I felt somewhat sick, but swallowed it down. I heard footsteps in the hall, tramping on the bare linoleum. Two black-suited men went past, carting a stretcher with a covered body on it. The undertakers. I wasn't religious, but my fingers automatically crossed myself. Uncle Toby briefly bowed his head. I turned slightly and reaching over the back of the settee, flicked one of the curtains aside to peep out of the window. There were several police vehicles parked outside, and groups of residents in their dressing gowns standing in doorways or peering through windows at the activity.

"Do they know Mrs Norris has been murdered?" I asked.

"Some of them," Uncle Toby answered. "The rest will either guess, or hear the gossip. We'll talk to the immediate neighbours now, then a house-to-house tomorrow morning. No sense in waking those who are not already awake."

"But one of them could be the killer!" I protested.

"Indeed, one of them could." My uncle sat down in one of the armchairs, crossed his right leg over his left. I hid a tentative, tired, smile. His striped pyjamas were showing beneath his trousers.

"But what if he gets away?" I added, concerned, the small smile of brief amusement fading.

"He? This could as easily be a she."

I wrinkled my nose, shook my head. "No, you'd need quite a bit of strength to crash that mirror down on her head."

"Would you?"

"You would."

He nodded, sat thinking for a moment, then asked me to tell him exactly what I had seen.

"Surely, Laurie, I mean DC Walker, has told you?"

Uncle Toby nodded again, "He has, but I would like to hear what you have to say."

"Oh. Oh, I see." I steepled my fingers together and pressed them against my lips, thinking. Aunt Madge always did the same thing, I suppose I had picked it up from her.

"We were walking home from the cinema, about ten forty-five? I'm not sure what time the film finished. We said goodnight to a man and his dog. A Golden Labrador."

"Can you describe this man?"

I bit my lip, shrugged. "Sorry, I didn't really notice; about your height. Hat, coat. I was looking at the dog. He couldn't be the murderer though; he has a dog."

I saw Uncle grimace. "Herr Hitler had Blondi, a favourite German Shepherd. He tested the cyanide pills that Himmler'd given him on her to make sure they worked before he committed suicide."

I took his point. Changed the subject. "A woman was pushing a pram with a baby girl asleep in it. She was going to the corner shop to buy powdered milk."

"What did she look like?"

"The baby? I don't know she was under a blanket and the pram hood was pulled up. One of those old carriage prams, not a push-chair; you know, like the one I had when I was little, for my dollies."

Uncle Toby laughed. I think he welcomed a pleasant memory from the past to shield the unpleasantness of the present. "I don't seem to recall you pushing dollies around in it, you abandoned those and subjected Martha, our cat, to wearing a lace bonnet and trundling *her* up and down the garden path. Poor old puss!"

"Poor puss?" I retorted indignantly. "She loved it. She was always curled up asleep in that pram!"

"I don't think she appreciated being bumped down the garden steps. Nor being tipped into the fish pond that time."

I managed to keep the laugh from reaching my face. "I didn't tip her, I fell over, grabbed the side of the pram, and..."

"...Tipped the cat into the pond."

A piece of advice. Never argue with a policeman, especially a DCI who knows he is right.

Our laughter subsided. Patiently, Uncle Toby asked his serious question again. "I meant, what did the woman look like?"

I thought back, picturing her in my mind. "Harassed. Tired. She had a headscarf on, a print of pink roses. A dark raincoat. I got the impression that the baby had not been asleep for long, probably she'd been playing her mum up. The pram was old, shabby. The wheels were rusty and there was a scratch along one side. Oh, and one of the wheels squeaked."

My uncle jotted a few things down in his notebook, when he looked up again, said, "We'll need a written statement, tomorrow, but while you are here," he said, in that easy going, friendly manner of his that, unless you knew him, made you think he'd only just thought of asking a specific question, "have you thought any more about that flasher you and Madge saw? I meant to have asked, never got a chance."

To tell the truth, I'd forgotten all about him. I thought back to the incident in the forest. "He was standing very close to a large patch of nettles," I said. "You need to look for someone with a bad case of nettle-rash in a somewhat personal area."

Uncle Toby chuckled. "Might be difficult to check. We can't ask every young man in the street to drop his trousers."

"That would create a bit of a stir," I replied with a small smile.

Should I mention about Eddie's van being near the forest? It was now parked a short way up the road outside the house where he lived with his mum, dad and brother – we'd walked past it both times, on the way to the cinema and then back again. I didn't especially mind about getting him into trouble, he was the sort who was probably often in trouble anyway, but I couldn't hurt Gloria. So, I kept quiet.

"No, there's nothing more," I said.

Uncle Toby pursed his lips, glanced at his notes again.

"Well, thank you anyway. Anything else about the woman and the pram?"

I shook my head. "Not that I can think of."

"Well, you know where I am if you do. And where *you* should be, is in your bed."

A DAY OF REST?

Aunt Madge brought me tea and toast in bed at nine o'clock. I would have preferred a few more hours sleep, especially as it was Sunday morning, but when she told me that Uncle Toby had got to bed at four, and he was up again at seven, I felt duly humbled so washed and dressed. A drizzly morning, but it was only a ten-minute walk to the police station, so, armed with an umbrella, I set off. Few people were about; the faithful were already in church, and for the rest, the pubs were not yet open.

At the fire station, I dodged a puddle the size of a lake. Further on, King's Head Hill was easy to cross at the traffic lights, even though there was another huge puddle beside a blocked drain.

Chingford police station had the appearance of a grand Victorian house, not a modern police premises, although there had been talk of pulling it down and rebuilding it for years. There had been two stables adjoining it back in the 1880s, the Victorian equivalent of a rapid response panda unit – horseback transport at the gallop.

Outside, a group of reporters were sheltering from the rain by huddling under the chestnut trees, plumes of cigarette smoke wafting above their heads. Several of them looking longingly at the still closed King's Head pub. One or two glanced my way as I walked towards the police station, but dismissed me as inconsequential. I hid a smile: if only they knew I was the one who had found the body! A very small part of me was tempted to march over and tell them. My five minutes of fame! Then sense took hold and I kicked the idea out as a completely stupid one. I'd rather be famous, even for five minutes, for something much nicer, thank you very much. Like being the winner of the Booker-McConnell Prize, a world-acclaimed best seller or the writer behind a smash-hit TV series.

I hurried into the police station as another burst of heavier rain poured from the iron grey sky, and was greeted by Sergeant Tanner. As I walked in, he waved his hand towards one of the chairs, gesturing for me to sit and wait while he dealt with the man haranguing him.

"It isn't good enough; I want something done!"

Sergeant Tanner, I could see, was nearing the end of his tether. "Sir, I sympathise that it is most unpleasant to find a bag of dirty nappies in your dustbin, but it is not a criminal offence. I suggest you move the bin in question away from your front wall, so that passers-by cannot reach into it. Beyond that, there is nothing we can do."

"The entire road was awake all night, what with sirens, slamming doors and comings and goings. The place was crawling with police, yet you say you cannot investigate that disgusting garbage discarded into my bin? My property, Sergeant, has been desiccated! *My* property!"

I don't know how the Sergeant kept a straight face at the blatant malapropism. I recognised the man; he was Eddie Jones' father. Same hair, same build.

Mr Jones tossed his hands in the air in exasperation and turning on his heel, headed for the door. "I pay my taxes. I pay my rates. I shall speak to my M.P. about this!" And he was gone.

"You do that," the sergeant muttered.

"Was that Appletree Road he was talking about?" I asked.

"It was. Someone dumped a bag full of shitty – oh, excuse me, miss, – *soiled* nappies in his dustbin yesterday."

I frowned. Could the woman with the pram have dumped them? That was rather an assumption – I dismissed it.

Not for the first time I pondered whether having children was worth the hard work. Did it depend on the quality and amount of support from the father? My pondering slipped sideways into wondering why Aunt Madge and Uncle Toby did not have children of their own. I was pleased because I enjoyed being an 'only', but how did they feel about it? None of my business, of course, but I still wondered as I dutifully gave my official statement and fingerprints.

Sunday dinner was always, without fail, at one o'clock. Usually, Uncle Toby was at home on a Sunday, for he firmly believed that everyday policework remained as everyday except Sunday. Reports to type up, reports to read, routine things to be done routinely were accomplished during the week. Murders, however, were not everyday, but Sunday roast dinner was still Sunday roast dinner, and as Uncle said, a man had to eat, even if he was investigating a murder. Although, he wasn't being as flippant as that sounds. With no useful information from a preliminary house-to-house enquiry, and no relevant reports returned yet, there was nothing new for him to go on. TV cop shows, like the popular *Z Cars* and good old Jack Warner in *Dixon Of Dock Green*, with Police Constable Dixon's catch phrase of, 'Evenin' all', gave the impression that police officers solved crime in a matter of days by working around the clock seven days a week. (Or even *Eight Days A Week* if you followed the Beatles' hit song!)

"Lay the table for four," Madge said when I offered to help in the kitchen. "Toby will be bringing that nice young man back with him. Poor soul looked dead on his feet this morning, and I doubt he has had a decent meal since he's been in London. Apart from the goings-on, did you have a nice time last night? Oh, and Rajah has lost a shoe, I'll have to get the blacksmith out as soon as I can."

I had to smile; Madge was adept at flitting from one subject to another almost in the same breath. It was her artistic nature; she was a painter – of watercolours, not the house-decorating kind. She'd been exhibited in a top London gallery twice, and her paintings of landscapes were always in demand. She had a studio up in the converted attic, where she would disappear to when the mood took her. Maybe that was why her paintings were so sought after – they were rare because 'the mood' usually only took her four times a year, her 'Seasonal State', as Uncle Toby and I called it. To be fair, her need to paint could last for weeks, during which time she would turn out a whole stack of new, wonderful pictures. I liked her watercolours, they were delicate and had an ethereal, mystical touch to them. They made me feel like I wanted to walk through the woods she created, or follow the track through a meadow, jump over the waves on a beach, or stroll beside a river to see what was round the bend.

We had several of her favourites hanging in various rooms around the house, the paintings she could not bear to part with for various reasons. The watercolour of a wild, heather-clad moorland took pride of place in the hall, and it immediately took Laurie's eye as he walked in with Uncle Toby.

"I say," he said, peering at it to study the superb detail, "isn't that Exmoor?"

Madge preened, delighted at her work being recognised. "It certainly is. Summer on Dunkery Beacon. If I recall, I painted it on the only day it didn't rain."

Uncle Toby put his arm around her waist and kissed her cheek. "And if I recall, you fussed over getting it right for the entire rest of the week, even though it was our honeymoon."

Madge batted him with the tea towel that she had in her hand. "Don't exaggerate. And open that bottle of red wine you got the other day, will you? It'll go nicely with the beef."

It did as well, although Aunt Madge and I drank most of it. Uncle Toby had only one small glass, and Laurie asked for water as he would be driving the car in the afternoon. I think he said this with a slight question in his voice, hoping Uncle Toby would give him the afternoon off – no such luck, unfortunately. Sunday or no Sunday, if evidence came in, they would need to be available – and sober – to deal with it. Would Laurie have treated himself to a glass – driving or no driving – if Uncle Toby hadn't been present? We made up for his lack of wine by giving him several more slices of beef, two extra roast potatoes, and a generous helping of apple crumble and custard for pudding. I think, hope, he appreciated it!

Talk over coffee turned to 'the latest incident', as Madge termed all Uncle Toby's more important cases.

"That poor old lady. Had she any family?" Madge asked, pouring a generous amount of cream into her coffee.

"House-to-house hasn't been all that forthcoming. Even so, we have established that she had a daughter and grandchildren, but no one knows where they are. We need to trace them, but, as we haven't found an address book or any letters, it won't be easy. Mrs Norris herself was widowed in 1959. Ex-RAF pilot," Uncle stated.

"And having difficulties with money. Living on a small pension that didn't go far," I added, thinking of the food coupons she cut out.

"On the contrary," Laurie said, "we found her bank book, an account at Barclays. On Friday morning she withdrew two hundred pounds, leaving as much again in the account."

I gaped at him, open-mouthed. That was a lot of money. More than I earned in a month. "But she always gave the impression that she was poor, even penniless! The food coupons, her house looking like a fifty's film set? What did she need the money for, I wonder?"

"No idea," Uncle Toby said, "there was no sign of any of it."

"Perhaps she paid off a bill, or something?" Madge suggested. "Electricity or gas?"

"For that amount? One old lady living on her own?"

"Besides," Laurie added to my uncle's words, "we found all her utility statements, neatly stored in the bread bin." He laughed at my puzzled frown. "It's not so daft, my gran does the same thing. She maintains that if there was a fire, the important documents would not burn inside a metal container. A bread bin is a nice size and shape to store paperwork in."

"Perhaps the money is hidden somewhere?" Madge suggested. "Under the mattress, or in a tin above the toilet cistern?"

Again, Uncle Toby shook his head. "Afraid not. We've had a thorough search. No sign of it."

"Was there nothing in her handbag?" I said.

Both men looked at me as if I had grown a second head.

"She always had it with her. A black plastic one that was supposed to look like leather. I know she kept a purse and her glasses in it, I've seen her take her glasses out on various occasions, and seen the purse in there. It's red with a gold clasp – again plastic. They sell the same ones in Woolworths."

"There was no handbag," Uncle Toby said slowly. "I should have thought of it for myself, few ladies can survive without a handbag."

"We don't have pockets like you men, dear," Madge said running her hands down her chic, close-fitting, pocket-less, cotton-print dress. She had a tall, slender figure and always looked good in whatever she wore. I envied her. I was short, inclined to being dumpy, (especially at Christmas when I stuffed myself), and had next to no dress sense. I usually went for comfort over couture.

"So, the murderer must have taken it?" I offered.

"Looks like it," Uncle confirmed. "Shall we change the subject?"

That was fine by me, as I must confess, I was starting to

feel jittery. Thoughts were beginning to stir. What if the murderer had still been in the house while I was waiting there? Or came back because he had forgotten something? I told myself, as I finished my coffee, that murderers did not go back to a crime scene. Or did they? My hand shook as I put my coffee cup back into the saucer.

Laurie noticed. "Are you all right, Jan? You've turned rather pale."

"I'm fine," I lied. "Just tired. Last night catching up with me."

"Let's take our coffee into the front room," Aunt Madge suggested. "I noticed you eyeing up my grand piano, Laurie. Do you play?"

Laurie's face lit up. "I do indeed, Mrs Christopher, though not since I left home to come to London. I assume you play?"

Aunt Madge waved her hand, dismissively. "I do, but not very well."

"Nonsense!" I interjected. "She plays beautifully."

My aunt pulled out the piano stool and patted it for Laurie to sit. He was obviously a little bashful, because he reluctantly lifted the lid and tickled a couple of the keys.

"I don't play that well," he said, running his fingers up and down the scales, "but I do enjoy conjuring a few tunes. It helps me relax, and to think without straining my poor old brain."

He tentatively played a little of *Somewhere Over The Rainbow,* then *Leaving On A Jet Plane*, and some of *Goldfinger*, *Scarborough Fair* and *A Taste Of Honey*, then he switched to Liszt's *La Campanella* and some Mozart, but he grinned at Aunt Madge and said, "This one is for you."

She laughed and clapped her hands as he thundered into a rendition of Russ Conway's *Side Saddle.*

We all clapped him when he finished with a flourish. I felt so proud – he was fantastic. Unfortunately, Uncle Toby had to break the party up.

"Time to get back to work, I'm afraid. And you, young

lady, get yourself up to bed for a lie down. I don't expect to see you again until supper time."

I waved his concern away and walked with them both to the front door. Laurie got the chance to whisper, "I might be busy this week, but I won't forget that I owe you a meal at a posh restaurant."

I smiled at him. "Don't worry, I know what life with a policeman is like. You concentrate on finding who killed Mrs Norris. There will be plenty of opportunity, afterwards, for restaurants." I was going to add 'and things', but thought it a little presumptuous.

When they had gone, Aunt Madge sent me up to bed. I had intended to work on the next chapter of my novel as I didn't think I'd sleep, but the next thing I knew, it was getting dark and Uncle Toby was knocking on my bedroom door, cup of tea in hand. He said that supper was ready; would I like him to bring it up to me on a tray?

11

BLACK AND BLUES

I dragged myself into work on Monday. Bad enough starting a long week after what seemed, despite the Sunday nap, a weekend of deprived sleep. As I got on the bus for the short journey along The Ridgeway and down The Mount, I felt like death warmed up. A phrase which, as soon as it entered my head I regretted. No amount of warmth would ever revive poor Mrs Norris.

By the time I'd stepped off the bus and hurried down Hall Lane, regretting wearing heels, and thankful that I had a pair of Scholl sandals in my locker, my throat was tight and my stomach was churning. Everyone would be asking me questions; questions I didn't want to answer because these would belong to gossip and sensationalism, not the 'helping with enquiries' police kind. And then my work colleagues would be wanting to know the extra, gory, details let slip by my uncle. It would be no use insisting that he *never* let details slip – gory or otherwise. At the thought of it all, I wasn't sure whether I wanted to cry or vomit. Admonishing myself to pull myself together, I breathed in a few lungfuls of air, and instantly regretted it as a lorry thundered past, spewing clouds of obnoxious exhaust fumes in my direction. So much for fresh air.

Doing as I had ordered myself; I squared my shoulders and raised my head – good deportment, Aunt Madge would have said, had she been there to approve – and walked with a brisk step towards the gate to the side entrance of the library. In through the open back door. I glanced at the clock in the staff room as I hung my coat up and shoved my packed lunch of cold beef sandwiches into the refrigerator. Five minutes past nine. I was late. Smoothing my skirt, short but not so short as to receive a frown from the head librarian, Mr Hurst, or a telling-off from his deputy, Miss Pamela Bower, both of whom, I swear, still thought that women should wear Victorian-length dresses. I smiled as I slid behind the U-shaped counter and thrust my handbag onto the bottom shelf beneath the reserved books awaiting collection by borrowers who had requested them. To my relief, Mr Hurst and Miss Bower were in the office. (To be fair, we did usually call her Pamela, but I would never have dreamed of calling Mr Hurst anything else; in fact, I didn't *know* his Christian name.)

The door was open, but even closed I would have heard most of what Mr Hurst was ranting on about because his voice was raised to parade ground altitude. He was shouting about being harangued by the police on a Sunday – a *Sunday* (his emphasis, not mine), regarding nuisance old biddies stealing – *stealing* – coupons from our – *our* – newspapers! I listened for a few minutes, one ear cocked.

"And then!" His voice was rising to a shriller indignation, "And *then*, the impertinent young man actually said – *actually said* – was I angry about the cut-out coupons because *I* wanted them! The nerve of it! To suggest that *I* need a shilling's worth of food coupons!"

I grinned at Pamela's reply.

"Don't you mean five new pence, Mr Hurst? We went decimal back in February."

I'm surprised he didn't apoplectically explode, but he probably wasn't listening to her. He rarely listened to anyone.

"If the woman was not, most conveniently, dead, I would have her arrested for theft!"

Miserable basket, I thought.

"Come to that, if I had caught her defacing our property – yes, Miss Bower, *defacing our property*, I would have considered killing her myself!"

I don't think he meant that, but he was in a rage and it sounded ominous. Maybe it was all bluster, but equally, maybe he *had* known about the coupons, followed her home and 'did her in' as they say in the gangster films. Nonsense, of course. I realised I had better make myself scarce, because if Mr Hurst had an inkling that I had arrived late, I would be on the receiving end of another of his tediously long and boring lectures about the importance of timekeeping.

I hurried to catch up with the girls who were finishing shelving the books left on the trolley from Saturday. There were six non-fiction tomes needing putting away. I sorted them into Dewey order, and with the pile in the crook of my arm, set off up the library. I could hear muted laughter from the area of the 640s, 'Household and Cookery', so went to investigate.

"You're going to be for it!" Trish said when she saw me. "Hurst the Worst is on the warpath regarding Mrs Norris cutting out those coupons. Apparently, he didn't know anything about it."

"We're not sure if he's got his knickers in a twist because he didn't know, or because the police had the *audacity* to ruin his *Sunday* afternoon."

"So, what's it got to do with me?" I protested.

"Your uncle and his shotgun sidekick were the ones who disturbed him."

I shoved two cookery books in where they belonged on the shelf. "Still nothing to do with me."

"Well, he *is* your uncle. You must know some of the detail? I mean, how often do we have a murder here in boring

Chingford?" That was Gail, my age but twice the bust size and half the skirt length.

"Uncle doesn't talk about police matters at home. It's his rule." I suddenly realised that, beyond the family connection to my uncle, none of them would have the slightest idea that I was there with Laurie when the body had been found. They wouldn't know that I had gone out with him, or know who he was. I pushed a gardening book in between one on roses and another on chrysanthemums, and gave my colleagues a sweet smile.

"All I know," I lied, "is that she died sometime in the evening on Saturday. Beyond that, we'll have to wait for the local paper to come out on Friday."

It also occurred to me that there had been no reporters hanging around that first night, although there had been those gathered outside the police station yesterday morning, and surely, they had not *all* been from the local Guardian? I thought I would have a look through the nationals at tea break to see if there was anything reported in those.

We were interrupted by Gloria joining us. She was usually late, but unlike me, took no notice of Mr Hurst's pompous blustering.

"What happened to you!" we all blurted at once on seeing the most spectacular shiner of a black eye.

"This?" she laughed and pointed to the vivid bruising. "We were at an invitation-only party Saturday night, dancing until the early hours at the Queen's Wood Golf Club. '60s stuff, the *Twist* and then the *Loco-Motion*." She did a few steps of the latter, pumping her arms like a steam train. "Eddie The Idiot was showing off as usual, he was in front of me in the line, brought his elbow back and smacked me right in the mince pie. It looks worse than it feels."

"I don't know about that!" I said, "it looks more than worse!"

"Like you've done a round with Muhammad Ali!" Trish added.

"Have you put ice on it?" Clara asked, peering closer through her glasses.

Gloria laughed. "Yeah, we fished the ice cubes out of my Coke. All that did was make me sticky."

"Are we going to do any work today?" Mr Hurst suddenly appeared around the corner of the shelves. "Or are we just going to stand here and gossip?"

We all mumbled various apologies and scuttled off, except for Gloria.

"I was showing them my war-wound, Mr H."

A few grunts and clearing-the-throat coughs. "War wounds are not to be smirked at, young lady. I saw *real* wounds when I fought in the war. Ah yes, shrapnel, the big guns. It was no picnic in the desert, you know, even with Monty cheering us on. We did our duty and fought for our country."

"But you weren't wounded, were you Mr H? I thought you were only in the ACC, the Army Catering Corps? Safe behind the vats of peeled spuds and boiled cabbage?"

Another grunt. Then, "I will not have you out here in public looking like that. I will alter the rota. When we open you will go into the office, I believe there is a backlog of overdues to be written out."

"Suits me," Gloria said with a shrug. She caught me watching from another line of shelves and winked with her good eye.

Unfortunately, Mr Hurst also saw me.

"Get that shelving done, Miss Christopher," he snapped, "this is not a mother's meeting house!"

12

TROUBLE IN THE NEWS

Half an hour of tidying shelves was long enough to do some serious thinking. One of those 'automatic' daily chores, making sure that the books were in order and looked neat. Why borrowers cannot put a book back where they got it from, and the right way round, is beyond me. We all had our own sections to do and changed round every Monday, so this was my first time on Fiction for several weeks. The A's and B's quickly done, I moved along to the C surname authors. Reaching *Christie, Agatha* I started wondering. If Gloria and Eddie had been to that posh golf club, how had they got there? It was on the other side of the forest, not far from Theydon Bois. (Say it 'boys', not *bwah* as in French.) No buses. They would have needed a car, and Eddie's van had been parked outside his house on Saturday night. Maybe they had got home early? Eleven-ish early? That wasn't likely! These private functions usually went on until midnight at least.

I felt uneasy. Gloria was lying, and it wasn't the first time she'd come into work recently with apparently accidental bruises. A month ago, she'd had a fist-shaped bruise on her cheek – I paused, the book I'd been putting into its proper place poised in my hand. Fist-shaped. Now what had made me think that? I pushed the book into its slot. Why? Because it *had* been fist-shaped! I felt awful to think it, but I didn't believe that Gloria had been dancing at a private party, or the black eye had been caused by accident with an over-enthusiastic elbow.

"Ten o'clock, ladies! I'm opening the doors!" The deputy librarian, Pamela's, voice jerked me from my reverie and I hastily completed that shelf and went back to the counter to look at the day's rota. I was on the public counter all morning, so wouldn't be able to speak to Gloria until the afternoon, and even then, I wasn't sure that I should say anything. But, as it happened, I didn't get a chance to chat to her about anything. Let alone a suspicious bruise.

An hour after opening, one of our regulars, Mr Garner, a retired gentleman who appeared every Monday morning to swap a pile of westerns for some new ones, and to read last Friday's edition of the local paper, came up to the counter to have his new books stamped out, and to return the paper – we always kept the local rag with us, otherwise it went walkabout and was never seen again. I had just returned from a fifteen-minute tea break, and, for once, the library was quiet in the sense that there were few borrowers in. So, I suppose you could say 'quiet' overall as well. Despite Mr Hurst's outdated preferences, we did not have the reputation of being one of those libraries where silence was the golden rule. Being on one level with the adult and reference section at one end, the counter and sound recordings spread across the middle, and the junior shelves at the other end, we did not have the layout for silence. (Especially when the schoolchildren came in!) Our reading area was one small corner with a few comfy chairs and a coffee table, so again, not suited for utter quiet. Great reading rooms like the British Library, or university reference libraries where readers went to study was a different matter. Oh, and I would like to add here, not one of us who worked at South Chingford Branch library had our hair scraped back into an unyielding tight bun or wore heavy, black-framed glasses as per the typical stereotype librarian.

Although Clara and Gail did wear spectacles, Gail's were a bright blue frame, and Clara's a rather fashionable yellow with black polka-dot design. My long, straight (nondescript!) hair I usually wore in a comfortable ponytail or a chignon.

Mr Garner had folded the paper so that page four was on top. He pointed to an article. "You seen this, luv? Your uncle said anything about it?"

Goodness, did everyone know whose niece I was? I had a quick look at the article's accompanying photograph, the police station. "I don't think so," I said, "should he have done?"

"Well, you have a read. Crying shame, I think." He touched his Trilby hat, gathered up his books and left. Curious, and as there was no one around to need assistance, I read the short article. It seemed that approval had finally been made to pull down the old police station and build something new and modern instead. I wasn't sure if Mr Garner was upset because of losing the old building, or the enormity of the estimated cost. It was rather a 'phew!' sum.

"And what, young lady, do you think you are doing?"

I jumped. Mr Hurst was standing right behind me, hands on hips, army frown creasing his stern face.

I indicated the article. "Mr Garner pointed this out to me. They are to get on with building the new police station at last."

"And since when has it been permissible for staff to read the newspaper at the counter while Joe and Josephine Public are waiting to be served?"

I looked around. Not a soul in sight.

"I will not have tardiness. You are here to work, not dilly-dally and shilly-shally. Nor do I pay you to read the paper." ('He' didn't pay me; the local council did.) "I have told you about this before." (He hadn't.) "I am not having it. I will be reporting this matter to the chief librarian, and you can explain your unacceptable, lazy, behaviour to him. I would not be surprised that he will then seriously consider letting you go. I shall be recommending that he does so. Now, get on with your work." He harrumphed, turned on his heel as if he were an army major, and marched off into his office, slamming the door behind him.

I was stunned. Was he threatening me with the sack? Just for reading a newspaper? Suddenly, all the unpleasant events of the weekend overwhelmed me. I felt my throat tighten and tears brim from my eyes. I was shaking and everything started spinning. Someone came into the library and up to the counter. I couldn't move. The tears began to cascade down my cheeks.

"Hey? What's this? I thought you would be pleased to see me – not burst into tears?"

I looked up, straight into DC Laurie Walker's kind, grey eyes.

"Oh, Laurie!" I gulped, and the entire sordid, last straw, episode with Mr Hurst gushed from me along with a flood of more tears.

A lady came up to the counter with three romances to take out. She looked at me, looked at Laurie and said with a firm, single nod of her head, "He's always bullying the girls, that one. Has no respect for the hard work they do. It's about time someone took him down a peg or two."

Laurie made no reply but fished a clean white handkerchief from his trouser pocket, and handed it to me. "Dry your eyes, blow your nose, then go and get your coat."

"I can't," I protested, "it's still half an hour until lunch break."

Trish appeared and stamped the lady's books out. Her eyes were wide and round, I knew she was itching to ask who Laurie was. He anticipated her by producing his warrant card.

"Detective Constable Walker. May I speak with your librarian please?"

Speechless, Trish nodded and trotted over to Mr Hurst's

office, knocked on the door, opened it. "The police are here to see you, Mr Hurst."

His grumble was loud and – grumbling. "*Again*? I have better things to do..."

Laurie pushed past Trish, strode into the office and I heard him say, "Like bullying young ladies? We take a dim view of aggressive intimidation at Chingford CID." Then he closed the door. He emerged again a few moments later, winked at me and said again, "Get your coat, Miss Christopher, we need to take your statement at the station. Expect to be gone for the rest of the day."

I could feel everyone's eyes on me – staff and public.

I fetched my handbag from under the counter, went and got my coat.

"Is she under arrest?" I heard Trish ask.

"Just helping us with our enquiries," Laurie responded.

What enquiries? No one said it, everyone was thinking it.

I couldn't resist it, as Laurie, in gentlemanly fashion, opened the monster-heavy door for me, I said over my shoulder. "I was the one who found Mrs Norris. I'm helping to investigate her murder."

Laurie laughed as he took my arm and guided me towards where he had parked the Jaguar in Marmion Avenue.

"But I've already made a statement. Why do I need to make another one?" I queried as we walked.

"You don't," Laurie grinned, "I only called in to say hello, but you were so upset I thought I'd do my knight in shining armour impression and rescue you."

"Do such knights tell outright lies?" I attempted a weak smile.

His grin broadened. "When there's a pretty damsel in distress and an ogre to defeat, we get special dispensation where white lies are concerned."

No one had ever called me pretty before.

He stopped walking and gently pulled me into his arms.

"And you do look most dreadfully pale beneath that lovely face."

I gazed into his eyes and a lump came into my throat. "I can't stop thinking about her, lying there stiff and cold. All that blood... and then when Mr Hurst had a go at me, I..." That was it, I burst into tears again. Laurie tightened his arms around me and held me close while I sobbed.

"Come on," he said after a little while, "you're in shock. Let's get you home to your Aunt Madge. A chance to rest, and some peace and quiet is what you need."

It was only later in the afternoon, my feet up in the garden, reading an Arthur C. Clarke science fiction, that I remembered I'd left my sandwiches in the staff room fridge, and hadn't changed my shoes.

13

SUNSHINE AND SUPPOSITION

Aunt Madge insisted that I took a few days off work. First thing Tuesday morning, she telephoned the library to say that I would be back on Thursday – Wednesday being when the library was closed and we all had a day off anyway. I didn't hear the entire conversation, but some of the words consisted of 'upset', 'shock', 'considering an official complaint', and 'your insensitive behaviour...'. How Mr Hurst responded, she never said, but her grin was as curved as a ripe banana when she put the telephone receiver down. There were several people who had not discovered, until it was too late, that it was not wise to cross my Aunt Madge.

Tuesday morning I spent lazing around, but also wondering when I would see Laurie again. I had, briefly, when he had picked Uncle Toby up at eight-thirty, but all I got was a broad smile and a wave. They were busy, following unproductive leads – or in fact, as my uncle said when I asked him outright at lunch – virtually no leads at all.

"We've several sets of unidentified fingerprints, no sign of the money she withdrew from the bank, although she could have spent it on something. There is no reason to assume it was stolen by whoever murdered her, although probably it was, and that's all. Apart from the possible theft of the money, there's no obvious motive."

"What about the newspaper?" I asked, after inspecting some lettuce that Aunt Madge had picked from the garden to make up a salad. She had washed it thoroughly, but having been caught out once by a missed slug I'd almost eaten when I was nine years old, some of my acquired ritual habits died hard.

"Newspaper?" Uncle queried. "We found a few of the coupons she had cut out." He chuckled. "Would your Mr Hurst like them back, do you think?"

Uncle Toby had as low an opinion of that man as had I.

I laughed, but corrected him. "No, I mean the entire paper. She took it from the library and had one torn corner of it clasped in her hand. I saw it."

Uncle looked thoughtful, nodded. "You're right. We didn't find the rest of that paper anywhere."

"It was unusual for her to take the entire paper," I said, "and she left early in rather a hurry, quite agitated. I wonder what she had seen in that edition that had so upset her?"

"Mmm, hmm," Uncle responded in his usual, but frustrating manner. "I wonder?"

An hour after Uncle Toby had returned to work, Laurie appeared with a copy of The Mirror newspaper dated last Friday.

He grinned at me, as I was stretched out in the afternoon sunshine on the hammock that hung between the two sturdy silver birch trees in the back garden, glass of shandy on the table beside me, sunglasses on, shorts and brief T-shirt showing off my figure. Which I would like to say was neat, petite and curvaceous, but was, truthfully, dumpy with curves in all the wrong places.

"The DCI wondered if you could read through it to see if you could spot anything relevant to Mrs Norris. We've looked at everything – there are some worrying and some sensational articles, but nothing that seems relevant to our case. We wondered, as you knew her slightly, and," his grin broadened, "if you're not *too* busy, if you could take a look?"

I threw the cushion that had been behind my head at him. "I'm very busy," I said with mock annoyance. "It is hard work getting a reasonable tan."

Laurie laughed. "As pale as a pumpkin is all right by me." He waved, and left.

As pale as a pumpkin? Where on earth had he got that phrase from? Pumpkins were orange, weren't they?

I skimmed through the paper to see if there was anything obvious. There wasn't. So, I read it from cover to cover, including the sports pages. I am no sports fan, although I did note a piece by Phil Beal and his reminiscence about the Football League Cup Final at Wembley, when Tottenham Hotspur won 2-0 to Aston Villa. An event I remembered – despite not being interested in football – because Uncle Toby had invited friends round to watch the match on our TV and, as Spurs supporters, they had all been elated. Probably helped along by the amount of beer they had consumed between them before, during, and after the match.

I even read through all the advertisements. The front page was dominated by the sensational divorce of a pair of Hollywood celebrities, I couldn't see how that would bother Mrs Norris. There was a piece about the Queen attending the racing at Royal Ascot, and speculation of whether Mill Reef would make it a triple after his spectacular victory of the Epsom Derby and the Eclipse Stakes at Sandown. And a small mention of a new rock group called Queen doing a tour of England. I'd never heard of them, so skipped that, as I doubted Mrs Norris had heard of them either. Only one article about a missing baby boy caught my attention, but apart from the awfulness of it, would it have so deeply upset her? I concluded that perhaps she was into upcoming rock bands, after all.

Aunt Madge brought me a cup of tea. I sat up and swung my legs over the side of the hammock and showed her the article about the missing baby.

"They still haven't found him," I said. "The parents must be worried sick, he's been missing for several days now."

"Yes, a two-month-old boy snatched from his grandmother's home. A tragic tale. The granny was looking after him while her daughter went to have her hair done. When the poor woman returned, she found her mother dead at the bottom of the stairs and her baby gone."

I suppose it was because of Mrs Norris that I asked, "Was it murder?"

Aunt Madge shrugged as she sat on the garden bench to drink her own cup of tea. "I don't think so. The baby was in his pram in the back garden and the front door was open. I think they," (she meant the investigating police) "think Mrs Batewell, the grandmother, might have heard the baby crying, hurried down the stairs, tripped on some toys left there and, tragically, broke her neck."

"Ah," I couldn't resist saying, "but did she fall, or was she pushed?"

Madge laughed at my feeble attempt at light humour. "Sad – or maybe a little glad – to say, it is not our concern. Chingford Police have enough heaped on their plate without wondering about how other police forces are managing their crime statistics. Or not, as the case may be. Which reminds me, there have been two more sightings of flashers in our part of the woods. Don't go walking or riding on your own, will you?"

Which was rather unnecessary advice as I didn't walk or ride alone anyway, but I appreciated her concern.

"I hope you take the same advice?" I said sternly.

Madge got up, collected the empty cups. "I never ride alone, you know that. I like the pleasure of company and the chance of a good gossip."

That she did, but she also rode alone if there was no one to go out with, riding one horse and leading the other.

"I'm off up the yard now, as it happens, Jan. Will you be all right here?"

"Of course, Dear Aunt. There are no toys on the stairs for me to trip over, and I doubt we'll get a flasher in our back garden. There is one thing, though," I said, suddenly realising it. "What if Mrs Norris was into betting on the gee-gees? Perhaps she read about Mill Reef – he was an odds-on certainty, after all. That could also explain the money?" I leaned forward, excited. "What if she withdrew the cash, put a bet on and won an absolute packet. Someone saw, followed her home and – bang! Hit her over the head to steal her winnings? I wonder how much a bet of a couple of hundred pounds would reap?"

"That might also explain where she got so much money from in the first place. A regular successful gambler?"

Just as suddenly, I was deflated. "If she was *that* good at picking winners, why did she need to cut out the food coupons? And her house didn't look very affluent. There didn't seem to be anything new for years."

"So, not a successful gambler after all," Aunt Madge countered.

"Maybe she was heavily in debt? Owed a lot to... whoever. She tried to repay some of it, but it wasn't enough. She argued with whoever she owed the money to, he, she, lost his, her, temper – and wallop."

"Reasonable suppositions, my dear, but if she were in debt to that extent why had she a substantial amount in the bank? Followed home by a thief after collecting her winnings is a good theory, though. I'll pop into the station and pass your thoughts on to Toby. Must dash, the horses need doing." She blew me an air kiss and was gone.

The conversation did remind me of two things: I wondered if the lady with the little girl in the pram had managed to get her powdered milk, and the matter of Gloria's black eye was still niggling at me.

There was not much I could do about the first, but I could do a small amount of investigating for the second.

14

A TELEPHONE ENQUIRY

"Hello? Is that Queen's Wood Golf Club?" It was. I'd got the right telephone number from Directory Enquiries, then.

"I was wondering," I said in my sweetest, cajoling voice, "whether you could help me? I was a guest at Saturday's private party and I think I must have left my purse there. It's a red leather one. Not much money in it, but I have a few precious photographs tucked into one of the inside pockets. One is of my mother and father who have now passed away." I put a little sobbed gulp into my voice. "I don't suppose you've had it handed in?"

"No," came the answer. Hardly surprising.

"Oh dear." Another little sob. "Could you perhaps give me the phone number of the hosts? They might have it. What...? Oh, no, I don't have the host's name or number. I went as a partner to one of their guests you see, and he is away on business abroad for several days now. He works for the British Embassy and I cannot contact him... It's most frustrating...You'll check? Oh, *thank* you. That's so very kind!" Phew, for a moment there, I thought I might have over-egged the pudding.

I waited only a few minutes. It was a very nice young man on the other end. Most helpful.

"What's that? Oh, you were closed Saturday evening because of a power failure? That must have been so very inconvenient for you – but did I say Saturday? I'm *so* sorry, I meant *Friday* evening!" I crossed my fingers. *Please let there have been a private function there on the Friday*!

There had. That was lucky. The young man kindly passed on an Epping telephone number for the party's hosts, which I pretended to write down, thanked him profusely and hung up.

So, Gloria *was* lying. She had not got that black eye from her boyfriend's over-enthusiastic elbow while dancing at a Saturday evening party – there hadn't been such a party. However, it was one thing to have established this fact, something entirely different for me to wonder what I could do about it.

Or even if I should.

15

WEDNESDAY WALKABOUT

Wednesday morning, I received a surprise telephone call from Laurie.

"Hello Jan, I've a few minutes to spare, so thought I'd see how you were doing? How's the tan going?"

I smiled; Laurie didn't realise just how much of a Devon accent he had. I loved the way he pronounced words: 'few' came out as 'voo', and he often rolled his r's.

"The tan is still as pale as a pumpkin and I'm a right *v*raud," I answered, "I *v*eel absolutely *v*ine." My smile widened. Had he heard me deliberately say 'vraud' not fraud, 'feel' or 'fine'?

"Good. Well, then, I've got the afternoon off and it's a glorious day. I thought we could go for a walk in the forest, maybe to that pub your aunt mentioned, the Owl? Have a bite to eat and a drink, then wander back?" It came out as '... afternoon ov ... vor a walk in the vorest'.

You can guess my enthusiastic answer. "Yes, please."

We parked where, last week, I had seen Eddie's van. I had still been wondering if I ought to mention my suspicions about him to Laurie or Uncle Toby, but as it was not there today, and I thought that I was being silly by making mountains out of molehills and all that, I shoved the thought aside.

We walked arm in arm, not striding out but neither dawdling, stopped to have a chat with two horse riders I knew and further on, to laugh at a squirrel scolding us for daring to be in *her* forest. Grey squirrels make the most absurd alarm calls, it sounds more like a rusted, squeaky wheelbarrow being pushed across a rutted path: '*Ee..ee..ee...eee. Ee..ee..ee..eee!*' And it goes on... and on... and on...

The pub was not full, being a Wednesday lunchtime, so we easily found an outside table and sat down to a wonderful Ploughman's of cheese, pickle, salad and new-baked bread rolls, accompanied by a pint of cider each. Laurie said the cider was nothing like the amber nectar Devon produces. "Drink a pint of Devin zyder and you'll be pickled vor the rest of the day."

Going back, we took our time, my arm linked through his, talking about anything and everything, including my dream of writing and his love of the piano. I mentioned the newspaper and my idea about betting on Mill Reef. Laurie said that DCI Christopher had instigated enquiries at the local betting shops, but so far, no joy. I privately wondered if we would ever, in some dim and distant future, get to the stage of Laurie calling him 'Uncle Toby'.

The cider had another side effect. I had visited the ladies loo before we left the pub, but to my embarrassment I needed to 'go' again. We walked on for a bit, but I was becoming uncomfortable, to the point that very soon the embarrassment would get even worse – and noticeable.

"I'm dreadfully sorry," I finally blurted out, "but would you turn your back a moment while I visit a bush?"

Bless him, Laurie didn't laugh. He actually bowed and made a huge show of turning away from me. I giggled and scuttled into the trees where there was a reasonable thicket screen and not too many brambles and nettles. Even so, I did get stung on my right bum-cheek.

"Ow!" I muttered.

Laurie must have heard. "You all right?"

"Yes!" I called back as I 'drip-dried'. "Just a nettle getting too personal."

I adjusted my clothes, turned round to scrabble back to Laurie – and there, beyond the trees in a small clearing was a naked man, his back to me, standing not twenty yards away.

I didn't mean to, but I screamed.

16

INTERLUDE: DC LAURIE WALKER

I ran. I leapt over the ditch at the side of the sandy-ride path, oblivious to nettles and brambles, and sprinted, head down, arms pumping, towards where Jan had pushed her way through the bushes, and towards the direction of her scream. A single scream. Then everything had gone very quiet – worryingly quiet!

"Jan!" I yelled, tripping over a tree root so I had to windmill my arms to keep my balance. "Where are you? I'm coming!"

I saw her standing quite still, her back to me, her hands over her mouth, frozen in terror. I grabbed her shoulders, spun her around to face me.

"You all right?"

She nodded, pointed with a trembling hand to a small, tree-enclosed clearing where, on the far side, the undergrowth was moving and branches were cracking. Someone scarpering.

I noticed that there was a tartan blanket spread on the ground and a pile of folded clothes, but did not stop to investigate. I charged after whoever was running away.

I called out several times: "Stop! Police!" although I often wonder if shouting out 'police' would do nothing more than galvanise any ne'er-do-well to hare off even faster. The old days of a thief or criminal stopping in his tracks to surrender, hands in the air with a resigned, 'It's a fair cop, guv,' went out of date with the Bow Street Runners back in the eighteenth century, and was only perpetuated in fiction and film, along with the remorseful confession at the end of an episode or movie. Confessions were, in my admittedly minimal experience, few and far between. Most who were arrested and subsequently charged clammed up and pleaded not guilty. Understandable, I suppose; who would volunteer to be banged up in prison for years when the prospect of a trial by jury could see them released? Until the day when we can gather undeniable evidence, too many cases get dismissed through lack of sufficient proof.

The trees were thicker on the farthest side of the clearing. Oaks, hazel, holly and hornbeams. No sound, now, of movement. I stopped to listen and to study the ground for signs of someone passing. Then I heard a twig snap and moved forward, cautiously. A figure dashed out from the shadows. I hurtled after him ... And didn't see the low bough of a very solid oak tree.

17

OUT FOR THE COUNT

I started shaking when everything went quiet. I thought I'd heard a thud and a muffled grunt, then, not a sound. Not a single bird tweeted or chirruped. The trees were silent with no breeze to rustle the leaves. It was as if the world had suddenly become frozen in time. Sometimes, when the wind was strong, the woods could almost sound like the ocean with a continuous *swish...swish* of movement rolling through the canopy. Not today. Today everything was holding its breath and listening.

"Laurie?" I called, softly. "Laurie? Where are you?"

And then a male blackbird flew out from the bushes ahead, clacking his shrill alarm call, *'Puk, puk, puk, puk'*. He made me jump, his alarm an indication that something, or someone, had startled him.

I was on my own. Should I go for help? But what if Laurie had been stabbed? What if he was lying injured, dying, bleeding to death? Or already dead?

I refused to think that! He was too young, too good looking, too *nice*.

"Laurie?" I called again. Louder.

Was that a groan? I walked forward, wary; picked up a stout branch and tested it by slapping it against my palm, although I had no idea if I would – could – use it as a weapon of self-defence. It felt comforting to have something solid in my hands, though. Just in case.

A moment later, I forgot all about blackbirds, stout branches and being alone as I saw Laurie, sprawled on his back, blood pouring from his forehead, unconscious. I thought that he was dead.

I threw my branch away, ran to him, panic sweeping through me.

"Laurie? Laurie! Laurie!" I fumbled in my handbag, a shoulder bag slung across my chest, for a handkerchief; pressed it against the cut, desperately trying to remember the basic first aid training I'd had when in the Girl Guides. For goodness sake! I'd won my guider's first aid badge, why the heck couldn't I remember what to do! What should I do?

Then Laurie opened his eyes, wobbled to a sitting position and lopsidedly grinned at me. Naturally, I burst into tears. Who wouldn't?

"If you ever, dare," he croaked, "tell a soul, and that includes your uncle, that I knocked myself out by colliding with the bough of an oak tree, I'll ..."

He didn't finish because I flung my arms around him and kissed him. I do remember that *that* form of action was most definitely *not* in the Girl Guide Manual. Nor the fact that he passionately kissed me back.

The blood had stopped flooding and was only oozing now, dribbling down his cheek, I refolded my handkerchief and pressed it against the cut, too hard because he winced and yipped.

"Ouch."

"I think that will require stitches," I said, wondering what to do. Then I had an idea. "If you can walk, we'll get back to your car, you can wait there and I'll run and get Aunt Madge. She's at the stables, they're only a little way further up the road. She'll have her car." Then I wondered if that would be enough. "Or do you think you need an ambulance?"

"No, no. I'll be able to drive myself, but we had better go to the station to report a naked flasher and what has happened, first."

The duty sergeant would take one look at the blood and immediately send for an ambulance. Was that a good thing? Should I go along with the plan?

I bit my lip, not sure what to say. Plucked up courage and blurted out, "I don't think he was a flasher. I think he was just minding his own business and taking advantage of a sunny afternoon to sunbathe. Nude."

Laurie snorted as he stumbled to his feet, using me and the tree for support. "Sunbathing? In the middle of these woods? In the 'altogether'?"

I shrugged. "Is there a law against nude sunbathing?"

"Not in a private place, no, but..."

I swept my hand in a general gesture towards the surrounding trees of Woodman's Glade. "We are on the very edge of Bury Wood here, but it's not exactly open to public view, is it? Very few people walk in here this time of year, it's far too overgrown. And he wasn't hurting anyone, was he?" I was talking a little louder than I needed, hoping that the man could hear me – I doubted that he would be hiding far away because of his abandoned clothes. He couldn't go far in his birthday suit, could he?

Laurie was doubtful. "True, but we *are* investigating several reports of a flasher, and..." He stopped, swayed, closed his eyes and put his hand to his head.

"And?" I asked.

He took several steadying breathes. Opened his eyes, but remained clinging to the tree. "And there have been two reports of assaults of a, well, unpleasant, nature. We need to apprehend this man before 'assault' becomes something far more serious."

I had gathered my courage now, and with my panic gone, was thinking clearer. With firm conviction I stated, "It wasn't the same person as the man Madge and I saw. This man today was much older, he had grey hair and," I couldn't help it, I giggled, "and a wrinkly backside. His skin was all crumpled – it looked like his birthday suit could do with a darn good iron with the setting on 'steam'!"

Laurie laughed, winced, and again swayed.

"Come on," I said, taking charge of the situation, "you've probably got concussion and you're still bleeding. Let's get you seen to."

My arm around his waist, supporting him, we made our slow way back the way we had come, stopping beside the blanket to investigate. I rummaged through the pile of clothes while Laurie leant on a tree. When I found the driving licence tucked inside a leather wallet in the jacket pocket, I showed it to Laurie who grimaced and put it into his own inside pocket. I put the wallet back and left the clothes neatly re-folded. The owner was going to be very upset when he realised that his identity had been well and truly discovered.

I did notice, as I helped Laurie into the driver's seat of his car, that Eddie Jones' rear-door psychedelic-painted van was parked further down the road, but I had no time to think about it as Laurie's face was most exceedingly pale.

"Drive down to the stable yard," I ordered in my most commanding voice. (Actually, this was the first occasion I had used it, I wasn't even aware that I *had* a commanding voice!)

To my utter surprise, Laurie did as he was told without argument. Which was not really because of my unexpected bossiness, but more to do with the fact that he realised he did not feel at all well, and it would be dangerous to drive on busy roads, whereas the stable yard and Aunt Madge were only about two hundred yards away.

18

CASUALTY – AND A NOT SO CASUAL CONVERSATION

Aunt Madge drove us to casualty at Whipps Cross Hospital, where Laurie had four stitches in his forehead and a tetanus jab in his backside, but was otherwise passed as healthy enough. He had a headache, but didn't seem to be concussed any longer. Even so, Aunt Madge tried to insist that he came home with us to stay the night in order to keep an eye on him, just in case, but he was equally as insistent that he would be fine in his own room at the section house. In the end, they compromised: Laurie would pick his car up, follow us home and stay for the evening, and something to eat at supper time. Except, Laurie adamantly insisted that he needed to put a report in to DCI Christopher before he did anything else. Aunt Madge was as adamant that Mohammed could quite easily come to the mountain, so, as soon as the three of us got home, my aunt telephoned her husband, explained the situation and he joined us as soon as he could get away from the police station – which turned out to be within ten minutes. (Driving himself. He was quite capable of driving, but preferred to be chauffeured around by his bagman. He claimed that it gave him time to think on things while not having to concentrate on the road ahead. I was secretly convinced that the real reason was so that he could have a forty-winks cat-nap whenever he wanted one.)

I made a pot of tea while the two policemen talked privately in lowered voices in the front room, then Uncle Toby came out into the hall and put his hat and coat on again, waving aside the tea that Aunt Madge had in her hand.

"Duty calls," he explained, "I need to deal with this *au naturel* woodland gentleman immediately, seeing as we have his driving licence, name and address." He looked at me thoughtfully. "I wouldn't object to some company, especially since my DC is temporarily making himself comfortable in our sitting room?"

He didn't need to ask me twice, despite Aunt Madge asking if my involvement was wise.

"She'll only be in the car," Uncle explained, "I would like to hear more of what happened, and she is a witness, if I need one." He peeped in at Laurie sprawled in one of the comfortable armchairs. "And as he's sound asleep, she'll not be required to do any nursing duties for an hour or so."

The sun had disappeared behind building clouds, the nice weather seemed to be drawing to a close, and there was a distinct chilly breeze in the early evening air, so I got my coat from the peg in the hall. Uncle Toby kissed Aunt Madge's cheek, winked at me, and we set off.

I enjoyed being in the Jaguar, the leather seats were like a lover's soft caress and the ride was smooth and comfortable. We did not have far to go, ten minutes at most to where North Chingford bordered the forest with a couple of untarmacked private roads, and grand houses to match the air of affluence.

Uncle parked, switched the engine off.

I said, "Obviously he earns a good wage to be able to live in such a posh house."

"Mmm, hmm," Uncle responded. "You know where the term 'posh' comes from?"

I shook my head.

"Well, so it is believed, the wealthy passengers sailing

84

from England to India in the days of the Raj could afford the more comfortable first-class cabins that were shaded from the heat of the sun during the long voyages out and back... Port side out, starboard home, which became abbreviated to P.O.S.H., and soon became a by-word for the rich and elite."

"I wonder if the posh 'gentleman'," I used the term 'gentleman' loosely, "who lives here knows that?"

"Shouldn't think so," Uncle said, getting out of the car. "His sort do not trouble themselves with the minutia of trivia. You wait here, unless I need you."

He opened the wrought-iron gate, walked up the crazy-paving front path and at the double front door, rang the bell. It was a little while before a man answered. Uncle removed his hat, and showed his warrant card. A few exchanged words, which I couldn't hear, Uncle Toby handed over what I assumed to be the driving licence, then went inside. The front door closed.

About five minutes later, Uncle returned, opened the car door on my side and gestured for me to follow him into the house. The man was standing in an expensively furnished lounge, with large patio glass doors giving view to a well-manicured lawn and weed-free flowerbeds that were in shadow from the lowering sun. I doubted that any dandelion or daisy would dare to contemplate showing even one petal for fear of immediate annihilation with the weed killer.

The man looked at me coldly. I was reminded of the hackneyed expression, 'If looks could kill'.

"As I have already explained," he said, tartly, "my driving licence was lost, I assume stolen, yesterday on my way home from work. I have not yet had a chance to report the outrageous theft. If you policemen were to spend more time *patrolling* the streets and arresting the troublemakers from the council estates, instead of accusing *innocent* bystanders of obnoxious allegations..."

"I must ask, sir," Uncle said, quite calmly, "where you were this afternoon at around the hour of three o'clock?"

"And, as I have already informed you, I was here, watching the cricket on the colour television set."

"Can anyone corroborate that?" my uncle asked.

The man sighed expansively. "As I have *also* already told you, no, I was here alone. My wife is attending a meeting. An *important* local council meeting. She is expecting to be elected as mayor next year, you know."

"Mmm, hmm, is she? No, I didn't know. That must be very exciting for her. Could you, um, perhaps tell me the cricket scores? Anything particularly outstanding about the match?" He smiled congenially.

"No, I cannot. I fell asleep half way through. I missed most of it."

"I see. A pity, I would have liked to know how England got on against Australia in the Test Match."

The man shrugged, although the expression that he darted towards me, was pure hatred. "I believe Australia won."

"Mmm, hmmm? It is a shame, but I doubt your wife will be elected as mayor. Not if it becomes public that her husband deliberately lied to the police when questioned by CID, wasted police time, and was subsequently arrested and charged with exposing himself in a public place." Uncle Toby cocked his head to one side. "Shall I go on? The Test Match – against India, not Australia – ended yesterday in a draw when rain stopped play. Lords, on the other side of London, was not enjoying the nice weather we have been experiencing here in the north-eastern suburbs. It was rather a good game, although a little marred by John Snow being in trouble, again, for throwing a bat at one of the Indian players."

I thought the man standing in front of us was going to burst a blood vessel or something, his face was so red. Embarrassment or fury? And I did not voice my query of how on earth did my uncle know about the cricket when he had been at work all day? The late evening news, yesterday? Although this was the first I had ever heard about him being interested in cricket. Football, rugby, yes, but cricket? He always said that cricket was a good, free, substitute for sleeping pills without the side effects.

Uncle Toby gave me a very slight, almost imperceptible nod.

I took up the baton. "Watching cricket is not your only lie, though is it, sir? You have not had your licence stolen. DC Walker removed it from your jacket a few hours ago. From the pocket of the jacket you are wearing now, in fact. And I recognised you, quite clearly, in Woodman's Glade." I folded my arms. "I saw *all* of you, Mr Hurst."

Mr Hurst glowered at me for a few seconds, then turned his attention to my uncle, dismissing me as if I were a Victorian child to be seen but not heard.

"I have done nothing wrong. There is nothing illegal about Naturism."

"Well, in one context you are quite right, but," my uncle scratched at an itch beside his eye, "if there is an absence of any sexual context or relation to nudity, and if the person had no intention to cause alarm or distress, then I agree, it would normally be appropriate to take no action, unless members of the public were caused harassment, alarm or distress."

"I was minding my own business in a concealed place..."

"In woods very close to a public bridleway, frequented by women, walkers and horse riders. So, not that secluded? And my Detective Constable sustained an injury..."

"That was nothing to do with me!"

I said nothing; technically, Mr Hurst was right. It was the tree that attacked poor Laurie.

Uncle Toby cleared his throat and continued. "There is still the matter of lying to a police officer, and in this case, such conduct of public nudity could be regarded as, at most, amounting to an offence under the Public Order Act. Regard needs to be assessed as to whether a prosecution is in the public interest. Given your wife's important status, such interest could be construed as being justified."

Mr Hurst began to splutter with indignation and anger.

"Prosecution? For *sunbathing* in a non-public area? And leave my wife out of this, it is *nothing* to do with her whatsoever."

I almost felt sorry for Mr Hurst when, at that precise moment, Mrs Hurst walked in. She wore a tailored coat with a fox-fur stole around her neck, despite the sunny day. I caught a glimpse of pearls at her throat. She looked very 1940s, I thought.

"It's started to rain," she said, peeling kid leather gloves from her hands. "Oh, I didn't know you had company, Egbert. Mr Christopher, isn't it? What is nothing to do with me? And who is to be prosecuted?"

My uncle acknowledged her presence with a slight nod, but said, "It's Detective Chief Inspector Christopher, and I think a prosecution, Mrs Hurst, will probably depend on whether the person who saw your husband exposing himself in a public location was distressed, harassed, or alarmed?" He turned to me, his head cocked to one side. "Were you distressed, harassed or alarmed, miss?"

I honestly do not know how I managed to stop myself from laughing. "I was initially alarmed and distressed, yes, given that there have been several perpetrators of obscene acts recently within that particular area of the forest. To come across a man in a, well, complete state of undress, was somewhat disconcerting."

"What are you talking about?" Mrs Hurst demanded, striding across the expensive deep-pile carpet further into the room like a Spanish galleon under full sail. "Are you accusing my husband of some ridiculous invention?"

"Miss Christopher, here," my uncle indicated me, "came across a nude male in Epping Forest this afternoon. My DC gave chase and was injured in the process. Aside from Miss Christopher being able to clearly identify that man, his driving licence, giving his name and address, was found at the scene of the incident."

Mrs Hurst stood in the middle of the room, her mouth

opening and closing, staring from Uncle Toby to her husband, then back again.

"A nude man?" she finally asked querulously. "In the forest? Unclothed? My *husband*?" The last came out like a cobra's venomous spit.

"I'm sure Mr Hurst did not intend to cause distress," I said, sweetly, "and he will ensure that he never does so again, in *any* form under *any* circumstances, to *any* one. He will not wish this incident to be made public, I'm sure?"

It was blackmail, pure, simple blackmail.

"What," Mrs Hurst said, quietly, coldly, furiously, ignoring me and walking up to her husband, "have you done now, you stupid, stupid imbecile of a pathetic apology of a man? You are back to this disgusting behaviour, are you? Well, I will not have you jeopardising my career in public service, I will not."

She turned to face my uncle. "Will you be pressing charges?"

I interrupted. "DC Walker's injury was an accident, and in this instance, Detective Chief Inspector, I do not think it would serve any purpose for me to make a complaint, or for you to take the matter further. I am willing to let the whole sordid incident drop."

My uncle replaced his hat. "Very well, there will be no charges on this occasion, but I strongly advise you to ensure that I do not have cause to reconsider at any future date, Mr Hurst. We'll see ourselves out. Good day."

As we left, we heard Mrs Hurst's raised voice and a resounding slap.

"Should we stay?" I whispered as we went out the front door. "Things might get violent."

"Do you want to?" Uncle asked.

I grinned. "Not particularly. I hope she gives him as black an eye as Eddie Jones gave Gloria the other day."

"What's this?" Uncle asked, concerned, pausing as we reached the car. I realised that I had spoken out of turn.

"Oh, nothing, Eddie caught Gloria in the eye with his elbow, that's all."

We could still hear Mrs Hurst tongue lashing her husband.

We got into the car and I burst out laughing.

"Police business," Uncle Toby said with acute seriousness, "is no laughing matter, my girl."

"Isn't it?"

"No."

"Not even occasionally?"

Uncle grinned. "Well, sometimes there's a reason to have a good chuckle. And maybe this is one of them?" He put the Jaguar in gear and drove off, grinning like a gorilla.

"Do you think she'll kill him for this?" I asked as I looked back over my shoulder. "She seemed very angry."

"I hope not. One murder investigation at a time is quite enough, thank you. But I'm pleased I'm not in his shoes. Mrs Hurst has the reputation of being quite the formidable dragon, and I rather assume, from what she said, that this incident is not the first."

After a little while, I said, "Poor man. No wonder he's always so grumpy. Fancy having to live with a dragon. *And* having the name Egbert."

"Naturism is important to a lot of people who follow that way of life, but it is not to be sullied by inappropriate behaviour in public places. The incident this afternoon is entirely inappropriate, so your Mr Hurst is not 'poor' at all. I could have thrown the book at him." Uncle slowed down as we approached the traffic lights showing red at the top of King's Head Hill.

"Egbert is an Anglo-Saxon name that goes well with the image of fire-breathing dragons, though, don't you think?" he said, still chuckling.

19

INTERLUDE: DC LAURIE WALKER

DCI Christopher filled me in with what he had established during his interview with Mr Hurst as soon as he returned to his beautiful house on The Ridgeway. After his brief briefing, I was very grateful to Mrs Christopher for the offer of a bed for the night, but I don't sleep well in beds I am not used to, so I politely declined. Not that I sleep well at the section house. Accommodation there is 'serviceable' – the basics without any hint of comfort. I would soon have to start searching for a flat or something, but rents were high, salary wasn't.

I also declined because I thought that to stay would cause embarrassment, for me, Jan and my boss, DCI Christopher. It's one thing enjoying the pleasure of a cup of tea, or a superbly cooked meal, in the company of very nice people, but quite another to meet them in the morning wearing borrowed pyjamas, with an unshaven face and bleary eyes. Aside from all that, my head was throbbing and I felt an utter idiot from knocking myself out on a bough of a tree.

As soon as I got to my room (the size of a large cupboard), I laid out the clothes I would need for the next day, and abandoned any idea of trying to get the stains out of my white shirt. Blood from the cut on my head had dripped down my face and marked the collar. Was it worth soaking it in salted cold water? That would involve tottering down the corridor to the small kitchen area, finding a bucket or a bowl and... When it dawned on me that I had no salt to use anyway, I gave up the idea and stuffed the ruined shirt in the waste bin.

It was only just gone eight, but I swallowed down a couple of aspirin, pulled the flimsy curtain across the single window that gave an unglamorous and uninspiring view over the car park, climbed into bed, and discovered that I couldn't get to sleep.

Thoughts kept tumbling around inside my head like a troupe of unrehearsed acrobats making an utter mess of their muddled routine. What if Hurst had not been merely nude sunbathing in a spot that he had thought would be private? What if he had more sinister intentions? What if he had attacked Jan?

I was already disgusted with the obnoxious man for the way he had shouted at her, how dare he? I had no patience for bullies – God knows there are enough of them in the police force, using the uniform or a position of authority to flout the law for their own advancement.

As for Hurst... We were already aware of at least three different men exposing themselves to women and girls in the vicinity of the southern end of Epping Forest, and following up an investigation into an assault that had been more serious than the sordid action of a man flashing his privates.

I was not sure about DCI Christopher letting Hurst off with a mere caution, though. Maybe 'naturism', as these people call it, is not illegal as long as it is undertaken in special designated areas away from general public scrutiny, but let's not beat about the bush here - nudity in private is up to the individual, nudity in public is unacceptable. I'm no prude, there is nothing to be ashamed of about the human body, male or female, but I do not approve of the recent fashion for women going topless. Although I do admit that attitudes change – not that long ago, it was regarded as risqué for a woman to show even a glimpse of a bare shoulder, or her legs, or even her ankles, an attitude that seems ridiculous to us now in 1971! Especially with the popularity of the mini skirt!

I lay there thinking for some while. Was my hostility towards Hurst nothing to do with his affinity for nudity, but all to do with his stuffy arrogance? And because he had upset my Jan?

That led me to a different train of thought. *My* Jan. I did, very much, want her to be *my* Jan. I had known her for approaching one week. One short week, yet it seemed, inside, that I had known her all my life. I was angry with Hurst because I was in love with her, with Jan.

There, I had hit the nail on the head. I was in love with the most wonderful girl on this Earth.

I turned over and fell sound asleep, a smile on my face and a glow in my heart.

20

TEA BEFORE TEN

Aunt Madge had tried to persuade Laurie to stay with us overnight in one of the spare bedrooms, but to my relief he declined. Don't get me wrong, I would have loved for him to stay, but goodness, the thought of meeting him on the upstairs landing first thing in the morning with me wearing no make-up, my hair all over the place, and in my Tom and Jerry PJ's...! I didn't think our blossoming relationship was quite ready for such a horror story just yet.

Waving to him from my bedroom window when he came to collect Uncle Toby on Thursday morning was a different matter – yes, I was still in my pyjamas, my hair resembled a badly made bird's nest, and I had not put on any make-up, but it was close-up scrutiny that concerned me. From an upstairs window, I was at a safe distance.

I leant out and called down to him: "Are you all right this morning? No headache or anything?"

"Only a bit sore because of the stitches, otherwise I'm fine."

"Well, you take care!"

Uncle Toby looked up at me. "I'll make sure he does, don't worry. I'll put him on filing."

Laurie pulled a face and I laughed. "Filing; the job we all love to hate!"

An hour later, suitably dressed, made-up and coiffured (OK, hair brushed, de-tangled and pulled back in its usual ponytail), I caught the usual bus, walked as usual down Hall Lane, arrived at the library, not as usual – ten minutes early. Only Pamela, the deputy-head librarian, was there.

"Oh, you're here!" she said cheerfully. That was also unusual, more often than not she was glum with that 'tired of life' sort of disappointed air about her. I'd always put it down to her being in her late forties and a lonely, somewhat frustrated, spinster. Which was most likely unfair, as I knew nothing about her private life.

Her smile broadened. I had never noticed before what a lovely smile she had. Actually, I'm not sure I had seen her smile before, not a *proper*, smile through the eyes and entire face sort of smile, one that comes from the heart and lights someone up from within.

"Are you all right, Jan? We didn't realise that you'd had to go through such an ordeal. It must have been horrible for you."

At first, I thought she meant my embarrassment at coming across our head librarian in his naturist mode, but then she added, "Finding poor Mrs Norris like that!"

She meant the murder; that was a relief. Explaining about Hurst the Worst *would* have been embarrassing!

She patted my arm and told me to take a break any time I liked if I felt I needed it, which was most kind of her, but this was beginning to feel surreal; Pamela Bower being exceptionally nice? Weird!

"I expect the others will pester you to know all the details – oh, here's Trish and Gloria now. Look, how about we all have a cup of tea in the staff room and you can fill us in with what happened? I'll put the kettle on, shall I?"

Astonishing! I had worked at the library for two years and this was the first time that Pamela Bower had given any indication that she was anywhere near human. Her austerity, her old-fashioned attitude, her fussing that *everything* had to be done correctly to the pickiest nit-pick, appeared to be quite gone. I started to wonder what had caused this sudden about-face, although I did have a very slight inkling...

While we waited for everyone else to turn up, I had a chance to mention to Gloria about her black eye – which was starting to look more of a lurid, splotched, yellow and purple than black.

"You're lucky Eddie didn't damage your eye, you know," I said as I opened a packet of shortbread biscuits that I found in the staff room cupboard.

"I'd do *him* some damage if he had!" she laughed. "And next time we do any synchronised dancing in a line, he can stand several feet behind me!"

"The party was at the Queen's Wood Golf Club, wasn't it? What's it like there? I've never been."

I managed to put a wistful tone into my voice. I had been there years ago when I was about eight. The occasion was a Christmas party for policemen's children and I hated every minute of it. I was never one for these sorts of over-organised parties. Other children seemed to enjoy running around screaming and playing those silly games – games where I was either last or the first one out, then had to sit and watch for ages while the game went on and on. I never liked any of the food, hated balloons (still do), and what put the tin-lid on this particular event, for me, was the Punch and Judy. How on earth adults think that the outrageous domestic abuse of Mr Punch is funny or endearing I have never figured. Ugh! No, thank you!

The last straw at the party was being made to sit on Father Christmas's lap. He was sweaty and smelled of what I now know is whisky. His lips were rubbery and he dribbled, so the kiss he gave me, on the lips, and his hand up my skirt to touch my knickers was not at all pleasant. (A child molester at a policemen's party? In the early 1960s no one thought about such a thing, because it was never openly talked about.) To cap it all, we were all given a present when we left. Mine was a shoebox size gift wrapped in red and white paper. I opened it to find inside, a doll. A really ugly doll. I didn't like dolls. I might have done when I was five, but not when I was eight years old. I preferred my large collection of plastic farm animals and cuddly soft toys, not dolls with those innocent, wide blue eyes that stared soullessly at you as if the wretched toy had murder on its mind. To add insult to injury, her head came off when I lifted her out of the box. Well, OK, maybe I should not have yanked her up by the hair and given the neck such a sharp twist.

So, all in all, I did not really have good memories of the Queen's Wood Golf Club.

Gloria shrugged as she spooned sugar into her tea. "It's nothing special, to be honest. The bar's a bit small and they don't allow women into the sacrosanct members' area."

"It's a bit far out of the way, isn't it?" I was racking my brain to think of innocent-sounding questions that I could ask her. "You've got to go by car, and that means the driver can't have a drink."

Gloria laughed. "Drinking while driving never bothers Joe... Jones, my Eddie Jones,"

She had been going to say a different name, I was sure of it.

She diverted attention by taking a cigarette out of its packet and lighting up. "And there are things called taxis, you know!" She continued talking while intermittently puffing out cigarette smoke as if she were an industrial-strength chimney. "Anyway, here's Brenda, so we're all present and correct." She raised a questioning eyebrow towards Miss Bower. "Apart from Mr Hurst, that is. Where is he this morning? Is he to join us?"

There came a couple of groans and a mumbled, "I hope not," from the gathered staff.

"Or can Jan tell us all without his harrumphing in the background?" Gloria added.

I will not be telling all, I thought, although I was, suddenly, very tempted for all to mean *all*. But I had promised Uncle Toby that I would keep my lips zipped about the forest incident, and a promise is a promise, although I didn't feel that Mr Hurst deserved the silence of secrecy to be kept.

Before I had a chance to begin filling them in about the ghastly events of Appletree Road, Pamela stood up and clapped her hands in a very school-mistressy manner. "Before dear Jan starts," (*'Dear* Jan'? Crikey!) "I have an announcement to make."

We all stared at her expectantly. Brenda, the children's librarian, paused while lighting up a cigarette to join in with Gloria's emitted tobacco fumes; Gail and Shirley stopped sipping their tea. Trisha neglected her biscuit in mid-dunk, and Clara ceased from stirring her sugar in.

Pamela cleared her throat. "Mr Hurst has had an unexpected family crisis, so he has had to go to his holiday home in Derbyshire for a few weeks to be close at hand with, well, with whatever it is that requires his immediate attention."

No one looked particularly crestfallen at the news.

"Has Mrs H gone with him?" Clara asked. Her dad worked as a caretaker at the town hall, and she often confided that everyone there detested Harridan Hurst as much as we detested her husband.

"I don't think so," Pamela said. "Mrs Hurst just said that her husband had been called away."

"Had a falling out, have they?" Gloria said. "Has Mrs H caught Mr H with his trousers down?"

Oh, how I wanted to laugh and say, 'Something like that!'

"It's all right for some, being able to afford two homes," muttered Gail, who I knew was struggling to pay a mortgage on her and her recently-new husband's small flat in Walthamstow.

"I think it was left to Mr Hurst by his mother when she passed away a couple of years ago. He decided to keep it as a holiday cottage, and a future place to retire to, rather than sell." That was Brenda. I didn't particularly get on with her, another of those who put on airs and graces and was adept at listening at keyholes to what she shouldn't be listening to.

I was still very tempted to tell them what the 'family crisis' was, but, apart from the aspect of my promise, it was all a bit too sordid to talk about, and as much as I disliked the horrid man, his personal preferences were not illegal if undertaken in private, or in designated nudist areas. So, until it was time to open the library to the public at ten, I recounted the events of Saturday night, instead, leaving out the unpleasant, gory bits, though.

One thing did make me wonder, however. Gloria, without realising it, slipped up a second time when she said, "We wondered what all the kerfuffle was when we saw the ambulance pull up."

The ambulance had come almost immediately when Laurie had summoned it (as a matter of standard procedure) at the same time as when he had called the police station. It had left again very quickly when it was obvious that an undertaker was needed, not medical assistance. So, Eddie and Gloria had either been together at home in Appletree Road, not out dancing until the early hours, or she had been elsewhere... with someone else.

Aside from that, at least one mystery had been solved. The reason for Pamela Bower's conviviality. Without the sour face and unreasonable temper of Mr Hurst keeping her spirit under his thumb, she had suddenly blossomed into a sunny, likeable person.

21

UNCOMFORTABLE UNDERWEAR?

The time sheet had me down to be on the counter with Gloria for the afternoon, her black eye concealed with make-up, but the library was busy so we didn't have much time to chat. (Although the general atmosphere was bright and breezy because there was no Mr Hurst prowling around poking his piggy snout into everyone's business.) One person after another seemed to be wanting to ask where different books were – honestly, did no one know their own way round the shelves?

I did, however, get a chance to ask Gloria if she knew where the young lady with the baby lived in Appletree Road. I explained that I had seen her on Saturday evening and that she'd looked upset and harassed.

"Aunt Madge came across a couple of lovely soft blankets that she doesn't want any more. They would be ideal for a baby," I lied. I needed a plausible excuse. "I wondered if the mum would like them."

"I only really know the people living near Eddie. Appletree is a long road, you know, not far off two-hundred houses, and that's without the blocks of flats at each end." She thought for a bit. "There's a baby somewhere near number fifty-three, I've seen the pushchair outside in the front garden.

Another a little further down – the house has a red front door and window frames, looks like a fire station. There's very young children in one of the houses down near the end of the road, the front garden is always littered with broken toys. And the corner house near us has a toddler. There's probably several more, but as I said, I don't know many people."

So, I hadn't got very far with my amateur sleuthing. I wanted to find the woman to offer some help; she'd looked so tired and end-of-her-tether-ish. I was also feeling guilty. I should have stopped to speak to her that night, I could have offered to run up the road to the shop to get the powdered milk for her. Could have, should have, done a lot of things!

"Oh," Gloria added, holding her biro up as if it were a magic wand, "there was a baby crying the other night, not far from Eddie's. Now, what night was it? Last Thursday or Friday maybe?" She chewed the end of the pen, thinking. "Friday! Eddie's dad was home early Thursday so I didn't go round, and Eddie picked me up Friday evening, didn't he? It was raining." She snorted. "Rare for him to do me a favour but he was on his way to get fish and chips for supper. Picked me up so that I could pay for it." She nodded, assuring herself that she had got it right. "Your uncle was waiting for you in that lovely Jag of his." She sighed, wistfully. "Wish Eddie had a Jag. Or a Lamborghini."

I didn't like to voice my thoughts that Eddie Jones was enough of a menace on the roads with a battered old van, let alone something powerful like a Lamborghini.

We always had a rush after school hours, first from Chase Lane Junior School which was almost opposite, then a little later, the senior over-elevens from Larkswood, or my old school, Wellington Avenue, flooded in, desperate for help with their homework.

One young lad, a polite boy of twelve years old, was a regular. He was an avid Doctor Who fan, as was I, although I had not particularly liked Jon Pertwee in the role at first. I always put any new Doctor Who novels aside for him, and it was rewarding when the lad's face lit up with pleasure.

"I haven't got anything new for you today, Gareth," I said, "sorry."

"That's all right, Miss, I don't expect it every time, and, anyway, I've got a school project I need to concentrate on. Can you help me with it?"

I nodded. "What do you need?"

"Have you any books on copper knickers, please, Miss?"

I stared at him. "Sorry?"

"My project is going to be all about copper knickers. I'm interested in that sort of thing."

Welding? Kinky underwear? At his age?

"I'm not sure that we'd have anything," I responded, hesitantly. "Are you sure you've got the right subject?"

"Oh, yes. Copper knickers." With great pride, Gareth showed me his school exercise book where he had written his project title down.

I creased up with laughter. "Oh! You mean *Copernicus*! The Renaissance mathematician and astronomer!"

"Yes, Miss, that's what I said. Cop-er-knick-ers."

I had the giggles after that until five-o'clock home time.

22

LABRADOR MAN

I decided to walk home. It was a nice evening, a playful wind that occasionally gusted from the south-west (the Devonshire direction), scudding white, fluffy clouds across a pale blue sky. Ideal for walking. I went the long way, which meant going down Appletree Road, along Waltham Way, past the council estate, and up through the municipal park to The Ridgeway. There were other, shorter, routes which I usually followed going *to* work if I didn't want to catch the bus, as these were mostly downhill and an easy walk. The reverse direction included several steep hills. The Ridgeway was called the *ridge* way for a reason! But my idea this Thursday late afternoon was to go in search of mothers with young babies. I thought I might knock at a few doors and ask after 'my' mother.

I figured she must have come from near or beyond Mrs Norris's house. The Jones family lived on the opposite side of the road in the middle of a row of look-alike terraced houses. We had talked to the man and his dog near number thirty-eight. I came to the house with the ornate fountain in the front garden, and smiled. Our first kiss. I wish I hadn't stopped Laurie from kissing me again.

Eddie's Mini van was parked outside his house (he never

seemed to be at work, that man), and I bit my lip with sadness as I noticed a few wilting bunches of flowers set against the wall of Mrs Norris's front garden. Police 'do not enter' tape was still stretched across the gate and front door as their investigations were not complete. I bent down to read a couple of the labels on the flowers: nice words from the neighbours. Abandoning my idea of mother and baby tracing, I turned around and walked back towards the shops. There was a florist near Rossi's, the ice cream shop, I'd buy something nice and leave my own contribution.

I decided on an attractive array of white, yellow and purple chrysanthemums, flowers which Aunt Madge would not have in the house as in some countries, she had once told me, they represented death and were used for funerals and to be put on grave stones. So not suitable for pretty indoor decoration, but ideal for my purpose.

I walked back down Appletree Road and, as I was squatting down to set my flowers among the other contributions, a man joined me.

I looked up, recognised him as the gentleman who had been out with his Labrador.

"Oh, hello." I said, getting to my feet, "no dog today?"

He frowned slightly, so I assumed that he had not recognised me.

"We passed like ships in the night the other evening. The night poor Mrs Norris was killed," I explained.

He suddenly remembered me. "Ah, you were with a good looking, tall young man?"

"I was, yes."

The man nodded, then he held his hand out for me to shake. "I'm Geoffrey Munday, I live down the other end of the road. It was a sad business, somewhat disconcerting for those of us who live here. We all hope that the police catch the perpetrator as soon as possible. Betty Norris was a dear lady, although she did like her flutters on the doggies."

I frowned. "Doggies?"

"The greyhound racing at Walthamstow Stadium. She spent more than quite a bit of time there, especially after her husband had passed away."

I was suddenly very excited. Of course – it wasn't horse racing she gambled on, but the dogs!

Mr Munday hadn't noticed my alert interest. "My daughter, Charlotte, and Betty's granddaughter, Cecily, were best friends from the day they were born in 1942, six hours apart in the same nursing home here in Chingford. It was one of those 'oo-er' moments when we discovered we all lived here in Appletree Road."

He bent down to read some of the tags on the flowers. "Irene, Betty's daughter, lived with her mother during the war, and when Irene's husband was killed in '45, she stayed on. She had two daughters by then. They were very different girls, Cecily and Susan. Susan was born almost at the exact time that her father was tragically blown up by a bomb."

"How awful!" I exclaimed.

He shrugged. "A lot of men died because of the war. Sons, brothers, fathers, grandfathers were lost."

"Women, too," I added. "My aunt's sister was a nurse. She went to Dunkirk to help evacuate the wounded. She never came back."

We were silent for a moment, reflecting on those who had given their lives, then he went on: "Charlotte and Cecily went through school together, then both were accepted for college – Girton College, Cambridge. The first university college in England to educate women. My Charlotte has always been proud of the fact that she went there, though we were surprised that Cecily's family had the money to pay for her fees."

I thought that a bit pompous, but let it go. "And what about Irene? I take it she does not live with Mrs Norris now?"

He shook his head. "Oh, no, Cecily married and went off somewhere several years ago, no idea what happened to

Susan. I think Irene moved to be near Cecily when the grandchildren started coming along."

Very tentatively I asked, "I don't suppose you know where she moved to?"

Mr Munday appeared puzzled; his brows furrowed as a shadow of suspicion crossed his features. Somewhat terse, he snapped, "Are you a journalist seeking background to a story? If so, you will get no information from me, young lady."

"Goodness, no!" I responded quickly, and laid a reassuring hand on his arm. "I only ask because I don't think the police have managed to trace any of Mrs Norris's family."

His eyebrows furrowed deeper and he moved a foot away from me brushing my hand aside as he did so. "And how would you be knowing what the police do, or don't, know?"

It dawned on me at that moment that I really was useless at this sleuthing lark. Time to make an explanation!

"The young man I was with is Detective Constable Walker, and my uncle, my legal guardian, is Detective Chief Inspector Tobias Christopher."

Mr Munday continued to eye me suspiciously for a moment, then he seemed satisfied. "There was another DI Christopher as I recall, quite a few years ago. He was shot, if I recollect rightly. He had a daughter, I believe?"

I answered quietly, "Yes. I'm that daughter."

His curt answer took me by surprise, and was more than hurtful; "Well, the police didn't succeed in finding *his* killer, did they? I trust they do a better job in this case! Good day to you, miss." And he walked off.

I changed my mind. Labrador Man, Mr Munday, was not as nice as I had thought him to be.

23

TEARS IN THE QUEUE

Deciding to catch the bus after all, I retraced my steps back up the road, abandoning the idea to walk home. Just as well, as the rain started to drizzle down and I only had a thin summer coat. I love England with our change of seasons, but I do wish the weather could be more predictable.

There were several other people waiting, workers heading for home, an older woman carrying a heavy bag of shopping, and two teenage girls giggling over the latest edition of *Jackie*. I was tempted to pop across to the newsagents and get a copy because the front cover had a very attractive young auburn-haired girl reclining in a rowing boat and wearing a very nice floral-print summer dress, while the text splashed across the bottom of the magazine proclaimed: 'The Paper That Puts You In A Romantic Mood'. Given that my feet were aching from tramping up and down Appletree Road, my romantic mood could have benefitted from a bit of romantic prodding. One of the men waiting was reading the *Evening Standard*. As he turned to a new page, I noticed the front headline, and gave an audible gasp.

"Oh, no!"

The woman with the shopping and two gentlemen turned to me with questioning expressions.

"Are you all right, duck?" the woman asked, concerned.

"The headline," I stammered, pointing at the newspaper, my stomach churning, "they've found that missing baby."

The man reading the paper folded it and proffered the page for us all to see. The bold, stark, headline read: '*Missing baby boy found dead*' accompanied by a photograph of an empty pram.

"Found him at Liverpool Street station," the paper's owner said. "According to this report, the pram was left between the rubbish skips round the back. Passers-by started to complain about a stench coming from the bins, but it turned out to be the poor little kiddie. He'd been dead several days, they reckon."

The shopping bag woman echoed my indrawn gasp of horror, although not the tear that trickled down my cheek. Even the two teenagers had looked up.

"Ah, here's the bus," someone else said as the red, double-decker number sixty-nine came trundling across the crossroads and pulled up at the bus stop. The man folded his newspaper, and went to slot it into his coat pocket but as an afterthought, offered it to me. I didn't really want it, but took it anyway, scrunching it into my hand as I found a seat downstairs.

It was raining hard as the bus drew to a halt some fifteen minutes later at my stop along The Ridgeway. I half hoped to see Laurie waiting for me with an umbrella, but that was silly, he would still be at work.

The house was empty when I let myself in at the front door. Aunt Madge's car was not on the front drive; I guessed she would still be up the stable yard seeing to the horses. Only Basil, the cat, was in, curled on the settee, one green eye opening slowly as I walked in and plonked myself down next to him. I'm not sure that he appreciated being scooped up and held tightly in my arms while I had a much-needed weep, although he soon started purring.

I felt better for a good cry. I made myself a cup of tea,

although I did consider a glass of wine. The tea won, I decided to have the wine later, with supper, and then resolved to get some writing done.

I was surprised, when I went upstairs to my room and sat down at my curmudgeonly typewriter with its aggressive 'A' key that persistently got stuck, to find that the words flowed from my imagination into my flying fingers. My main character, Radger (to rhyme with badger) Knight, had just had his spacecraft (*Excalibur XII*) boarded by the Intergalactic Police searching for smuggled goods. Their DCI, Anton Vassal, (I had decided to keep the familiar police terms, even if the story was set in the twenty-third century), was certain that Radger had stolen items aboard. He was, of course, a corrupt bad-guy cop. Radger, the good-guy, was being cool, playing with his five-year-old prescient daughter, Electra. His wife, Andromeda, a telepath, was busy surreptitiously sending telepathic messages to warn the rebels that Vassal was on the warpath.

Putting it simply like that, my attempt at writing sounds corny, but there are fight scenes, narrow scrapes and romantic moments. The fantasy, blended with the science and the action, was resulting in what I considered to be a rollicking good story that would one day be published. I hoped.

One can but dream.

24

A CASE IN COURT

I had to take more time off work on Friday morning as I was obliged to attend the Coroner's Court. My presence was required as the district coroner would, as my uncle told me, need to hear direct from me what had occurred, both at the library on the Friday evening and on the Saturday when Laurie and I had found poor Mrs Norris's body.

Did I really only meet him one week ago? What a lot had happened in those seven days!

I was slightly nervous about attending as I did not want to say or do the wrong thing; on the other hand, it would mean I would see Laurie again. To alleviate some of my nerves, I had taken out a library book to read about the history of coroners, information which I found fascinating.

The word 'coroner' came from a thirteenth-century officer, *the custos placitorum coronae*, responsible for protecting the royal family's private property. The role eventually changed into duties to oversee criminal justice. By the seventeenth-century, a coroner's main function was to establish the cause of death, and by the 1800s, the position was usually held by a man of legal status, like a solicitor, who was paid the grand sum of £1 per inquest, although in today's money I guessed that would be the grand sum of about £6.

There were no special courtrooms back then, so proceedings were usually held in a tavern or public house that had a large enough room to accommodate everyone attending. As with today, the only purpose was to reach a verdict on the *cause* of death – natural, accident or deliberate killing, but not to establish who was responsible for anything unlawful. Sitting in the courtroom next to Laurie, I couldn't help thinking that I wished we continued to use pubs – my throat was so dry, and I'm certain that everyone could see me shaking, so a stiff tot of brandy would have gone down a treat, despite the fact that I didn't especially care for the taste. I didn't like cough medicine either, but I still swallowed the vile stuff when I needed to.

Uncle Toby and Laurie both spoke with calm confidence, but then they both had accumulated plenty of practice. When it came to my turn, though, the coroner was most kind and immediately put me at ease, reminding me that this was not a court of justice but a legal opportunity to identify the nature of a sudden death. I spoke clearly, recounted what had happened and answered his questions as well as I could. My part in the proceedings were over in a few minutes, with the final outcome being 'death by the unlawful killing by person or persons unknown'. In addition, the coroner agreed to the police request that the body was not to be released for burial until such time as an investigation had reached a suitable conclusion. Given that, as yet, there was no kin to speak of traced or informed, this was perhaps just as well.

As we walked from the building, it was gone midday, and, to my relief, Uncle Toby escorted Laurie and me round the corner to the pub where he treated us to a generous helping of pub grub shepherd's pie – and a brandy. The pie was delicious, the brandy was vile, but both served their purpose.

I had related my encounter with Mr Munday to my uncle the previous evening, and he had been most interested to learn about Irene, Cecily, Susan and Charlotte. He was also irritated.

"Why did they not come forward with this information? We put notes through every letterbox where we didn't receive an answer to our house-to-house enquiries." He also swore under his breath. My uncle rarely used bad language, but I clearly heard him say, "Blasted bloody idiots."

It seemed he had traced Mr Munday's address that morning, and offered to drop me back at the library before he and Laurie called at the man's house to, hopefully, find out more details. I rather wished that I could go with them to listen in on my uncle remonstrating with them about not 'volunteering to help with police enquiries', but books and borrowers awaited my attention.

Laurie promised to pick me up when I finished at eight o'clock. So, at least I had that to look forward to.

25

INTERLUDE: DC LAURIE WALKER

Friday, yesterday, had started with the Coroner's Court, a straightforward, if frustrating, procedure. Frustrating because we had got nowhere with any clue as to who had murdered Mrs Norris, or why, apart from Jan's revelation that the old dear had enjoyed the dog racing, so that could be a connection. There was a lot of money to be made, or lost, at the dogs. But 'could' did not make much of a case, or help with genuine information.

I felt bad about letting Jan down on the Friday evening. She said, when I phoned her from the station, that she did not mind that I couldn't make it after all, said, as she had once before, that she was used to the complicated hours that a policeman had to work. I'm not sure whether she was genuinely understanding or just being nice; either way, I could tell that she was disappointed. Which was cheering in a sense, because it meant she had *wanted* to see me, although I had no way of knowing this was as much as I wanted to see her. The only comfort was that Mrs Christopher was in the same boat, for the DCI and I were both tied up with a case of attempted robbery that had taken place in the late afternoon. Two thieves had tried to rob the jewellers in Station Road, unsuccessfully, as they had not bargained on the bravery of the jeweller, or his newly installed automatic locking door. We arrested the culprits, but taking statements, booking and charging, all took its toll on the time. Like most policemen, I detest paperwork – I doubt this will be the only occasion you hear me say so!

Before that, the DCI and I had driven round to the house where Mr Geoffrey Munday lived, Labrador Man, as Jan called him. With no answer, we had headed back to the station. Half way along Waltham Way, we had stopped to see if we needed to assist with a road traffic accident that had occurred a few minutes beforehand. A delivery van had pulled out of a side road without taking due care and attention, and had slammed straight into an oncoming car. The car was a write-off, but fortunately the driver, a woman, at first inspection, had seemed unharmed, except for some bruising and shock. Even so, I had called in for an ambulance and requested a patrol car to attend. On our way again some half-hour later, we had just turned right into King's Head Hill when the call came in via the car radio about the attempted robbery, so that was it for the rest of Friday.

Saturday morning found myself and the DCI once again knocking at the Munday's front door. From inside, some furious barking, and then the lady of the house answered. Mr Munday was at work, but his wife was most informative and helpful, although she did announce that her husband did not approve of 'gossip'. She, clearly, did not share the same reservations.

"He didn't think we had anything useful to tell you," she said, when we mentioned that they should have come forward with their important information. I managed to hide my smile at DCI Christopher's discreet eye roll.

She confirmed what Jan had told us: Mrs Norris had a daughter, Irene, two granddaughters, Cecily and Susan, and four young great-grandsons. They lived somewhere in Cambridgeshire, she thought.

"Nice girl, Cecily, though the family was always hard up.

It must have been a struggle for Irene to buy school uniforms and such for the children." She lowered her voice to add, "Susan didn't go to the grammar school like Cecily and my Charlotte did, and we think that Cecily's university fees might have been paid by, well, you know, *charity*."

"Or maybe a scholarship?" I suggested. "Or a grant?" I could see from her expression that she regarded the family's financial difficulties as something to sneer at.

Mrs Munday pursed her lips and shook her head. "Oh, no, I don't think so. Betty gambled, she was always up at the Stadium. I expect that's why they were a bit short of a bob or two. Although, I guess there might have been enough winnings to pay for things. I'm not sure that money gained by betting is suitable for a Cambridge education, though."

Snobbishness. I hate it.

"We lost touch when the girls married and moved away," she added. "We never had much to do with Susan, she was not as bright or as well-mannered as Cecily. My husband often said that he thought she was not quite all there, if you know what I mean. Would you like some tea or coffee?"

I wrote copious notes in my notebook to distract myself from making a scathing retort of some sort. We both accepted the offer of coffee.

"It looks like our next stop will be Cambridgeshire police," the DCI said as Mrs Munday went into the kitchen to put the kettle on. "Are you up for the drive as soon as we've finished here?"

It was Saturday. I had hoped for at least part of the afternoon off, but time, tide, a DCI and a policeman's enquiries wait for no man.

We had been at the house for about half an hour when the telephone rang. Mrs Munday answered it, only to return from the hall to announce that it was a call for DCI Christopher.

Standard procedure to let the police station know where we would be; all the same, unless a situation was an emergency or important, it was not that usual to receive telephone calls while interviewing people in their own homes.

It was a brief call. The Guv hurried back into the sitting room, apologised for having to cut our talk short as he quickly gathered up his hat and coat. We thanked Mrs Munday, said we would be back if we needed any further information, or could she call us if she remembered anything more, and left.

Something was wrong, but I said nothing until we got back into the car.

"What's up, sir?" I asked, concerned, as I slid the car key into the ignition, and purred the Jag into life.

DCI Christopher's face was a grey mixture of distress and anger.

"Get us to the forest as quick as you can. There's been another attack. A horse arrived back, riderless, at the stable yard, covered in sweat and dripping blood."

My soul froze. My hands clamped rigid on the steering wheel as I stared at him. I almost could not speak. I did not want to ask, but I had to.

"Who was the rider?"

Grim, he answered with two short words. "My wife."

26

A TELEPHONE CALL

The telephone call came as I was shelving books. We were busy, as we usually were on a Saturday, men mostly, who had been at work all week. Pamela had been at her desk beneath the windows sorting out some book request enquiries – she had been really pleasant since Mr Hurst had disappeared. We were all hoping that the rumour that he would not be coming back was true. I had a feeling that it probably was, but I could not say so, otherwise I would have to give an explanation of how I knew. Deep down I would have given anything to rat on him.

Pamela came to fetch me. "Put those books down and get your coat, you're needed at the police station."

I gaped at her as if I were a stranded fish. Finally managed to say, "Why? What have I done?"

"Nothing, silly, but I've just taken a call. Your uncle needs you there as soon as possible – or even sooner. It seems that there's been an incident."

Laurie? Was Laurie hurt?

I dumped my armful of books back on the trolley and fetched my handbag from beneath the counter. Pamela was quickly explaining to the others.

"Is Eddie around?" I asked Gloria. "I have to get to North

Chingford as soon as I can. Could he give me a lift, do you think?" I was reluctant to ask as I really did not like Eddie Jones, but needs must in an emergency.

Gloria shook her head. "Sorry, no. He's out somewhere."

I bit my lip, tried not to cry. It could take ages by bus! "What if Laurie's been hurt, or killed, or something?"

Pamela was rooting beneath the counter for her own handbag. "Look, if there had been an accident like that, the message would have been for you to go to the hospital, wouldn't it? Not the police station."

"Maybe they've caught the person who killed Mrs Norris, and need you to identify him?" Trish suggested.

"They'd send a car for that," Gloria scoffed. I wish she hadn't, because Trish's idea had calmed me down a little. Now my heart rate was soaring again, and I felt sick.

"Come on," Pamela said, opening her bag and fishing out a set of car keys, "I'll drive you."

"But what about the library...?" I protested.

"What about it?" Pamela retorted giving a slight, indifferent shrug.

One of the Saturday girls had run out the back and fetched my jacket. She shoved it into my arms and pushed me towards the main door, with Pamela hot on my heels.

"Hope everything is OK!" one of the borrowers waiting in the short queue to return his books called out. I didn't get a chance to answer.

Before I knew it, Pamela was driving up Hurst Avenue and turning right at the top to come out just below the crest of The Mount – a quicker route than trying to negotiate the traffic further down where the shops were, even though we had to wait a couple of minutes before we could pull out when there was enough of a gap. Fortunately, a bus was slowly chuntering up the hill, its gears grating, holding everything up behind it.

From there, along The Ridgeway, past our house. I noticed Aunt Madge's car was not there. Where was she? Already at the station? Had something happened to Uncle Toby? I started to feel the panic rising again.

"Nearly there," Pamela said, reassuring me.

The traffic lights at the crossroads were red, naturally, so we had to stop and wait for them to change to green.

"Shall I get out and cross over?" I proposed.

"By the time you do, they'd have changed... Look, here we go!" Pamela slid the car into gear, drove to the road opposite and pulled up by the side of the station. I got out quickly.

"You take care!" Pamela called as I slammed the door shut and ran towards the main entrance, only realising as she drove off, that I hadn't said thank you.

About to push the door open, someone on the inside beat me to it – I collided with Sergeant Tanner who, rebounding, held out a steadying hand, and called, 'Whoa there, now. What's the hurry?" Then he saw it was me. "Oh, Miss Christopher. What are you doing here?"

I would have sobbed if I'd had the breath. "I was told to come here..." I panted.

"No, no," he said, taking my arm and steering me to the side road where a blue and white Panda car was waiting, engine running, a fresh-faced young constable who appeared to be almost my age, at the wheel.

"You're wanted up at your aunt's stable yard, not here," Sergeant Tanner said, "Come on, hop in, that's where we're off to."

He all but bundled me into the back seat, then got in the front passenger side, and slammed the door. Within minutes, siren blaring, blue lights flashing, we were making our way through the side streets heading for Bury Road, the forest, and the stable yard. It might sound unbelievable, given my family connection, but I had never been in a police car with the siren blaring. It was a little unnerving.

We skidded (figuratively, not literally!) to a halt where the forest ended and the hamlet of expensive detached houses of Hawkwood began. The cul-de-sac off to the side was jam-packed with police cars and vans, policemen, police women and police dogs all milling around. I wasn't aware that Chingford Division had so many on the payroll. (I learnt later that some had been hurriedly drafted in from neighbouring Waltham Abbey.) I spotted my uncle's Jaguar, and pleaded for Sergeant Tanner to let me out. I was running, dodging through the crowd of uniformed officers – and was caught by the strong, safe, arms of Laurie.

He was all right! He wasn't hurt! I threw my arms around him, and yes, you've guessed, burst into tears.

"I'm all right," he said several times, and produced his handkerchief from a pocket.

I took it, blew my nose. "I seem to be making a collection of these," I sniffed. "What's happened?" I managed to ask in a quavering voice.

Laurie took me to one side and sat me down on a front garden wall, mindful of a resplendent rose bush in full bloom.

I peered over his shoulder, "Where's my uncle?"

"He's somewhere down that bridle path. Your aunt has been attacked. She's missing."

"What!" I leapt to my feet, intending to run down the bridle path myself, but Laurie grasped my shoulders and plonked me down on the wall again.

"But how? Where? When?" I asked, my thoughts churning, nothing making sense. "She never rode alone." I bit my lip. She did, sometimes, although never let on to the fact to Uncle Toby.

"She wasn't alone. She was out with Kitty, is it? The girl who helps Mrs Christopher with the horses?"

I nodded. Kitty Darnell was the yard's official groom; she helped with the feeding, mucking out the stables and many of the other necessary daily chores required where keeping horses was concerned.

"The two of them were down the other end of this sandy ride, where it branches into another ride, I think?"

I nodded; I knew where he meant. "This is the First Sandy, that junction is the Second Sandy Ride."

Laurie nodded. "A man ran out from the bushes at the clearing by the junction and grabbed the reins of your aunt's horse."

"Which horse?" I asked, my voice trembling. "If it was Kaler, there would be trouble, he hates people he doesn't know near his head." We didn't know his history, but Aunt Madge had always reckoned that someone in his past had hit him, making him headshy. He also hated his ears being touched.

"She was riding the big bay, the scatty thoroughbred," Laurie forced a smile. "Scatty, being your uncle's words, not mine."

Kaler!

Laurie went on to explain. "Kitty says he reared, and your aunt fell off. He lost his balance, stumbled to his knees, scrabbled up and bolted. Panicked, the horse Kitty was riding – Rajah is it? – took off after him."

I put my hands over my mouth, I don't know how I managed to stop myself from screaming.

Patiently, Laurie carried on. "Kitty is in a right state, she says she tried to stop but Rajah just galloped after his friend."

"Yes, he would, he hates being on his own."

Laurie was rubbing my arms with his hands, he was as agitated as me, but was trying to keep professionally calm. "We've tried to reassure Kitty that she did the right thing to call us immediately."

"Where is she?" I asked. "She must be feeling awful." I was asking all the mundane questions because I didn't want to ask the important ones.

"She is, but she's seeing to Kaler. He's cut his knees. She has called the vet, but your uncle thinks that you should be there as you know the horse, and the vet."

I shook my head, emphatically. "Kitty knows more than I do. I'll help look for Aunt Madge." I stood up, thankful that today I was wearing slacks and flat shoes, not my usual short skirt and heels.

"I'd rather you went to the yard, where I know you will be safe. We don't know who this man is, or what he is capable of."

"Which is precisely why we need to find my aunt as soon as we can."

I brushed past Laurie and started to head for the gap between the trees that led onto the sanded track. Two police dog handlers were ahead of me, their German Shepherds straining at their leads. I lengthened my stride to catch up with them, then stopped abruptly, pointed (all right, somewhat theatrically), to a man about to get into one of the civilian vehicles parked further down the road.

"That's him!" I yelled, at the top of my voice. "That's Eddie Jones! He's the flasher; he's the one who attacked my aunt!" I was screaming now; everyone was turning to stare at me. "He's violent! He's been hitting Gloria! I know he has; I've seen the bruises!"

Laurie was holding my arms, restraining me; I tried to fight him off. I screeched, "What have you done to my aunt, Eddie Jones?"

My uncle had appeared from the woods and was quickly beside me, his hand also on my arm, his voice low and steady, calming me with nonsense words. I have no idea what he was saying, but the tactic worked.

I crumpled, found myself in his arms, sobbing against his chest.

"I know its Eddie Jones," I mumbled into his jacket. "I recognised him that day in the forest when I was out riding with Aunt Madge. He wore a mask, but I saw the bluebird tattooed on his neck. A swallow."

"You're sure of this?" Uncle asked.

I nodded. "I'm sure." I gulped a breath. Added truthfully, "I think."

I heard Laurie say that he would check it out. I tried to

pull away, was about to scream some more abuse at Eddie, but Uncle put his finger to my lips.

"Shh, shush now. Be a good girl and leave this to us, hmm?"

The next thing I knew, a WPC was gently steering me back to the wall that I had sat on, while Uncle went to join Laurie who was talking to Eddie Jones. They spoke together for a while, with Eddie agitatedly waving his arms around like a gale-battered windmill's sails, and gesturing towards his van and the house it was parked outside. Then Laurie went to the front door, knocked, went inside. A few minutes later, came out again. And I couldn't believe it – they were letting Eddie get into his van! He glowered at me as he drove past, accompanied by a crude gesture.

I leapt to my feet and hared down the road, yelling something unpleasant about Eddie. How he had hit Gloria, exposed himself to me and Aunt Madge, now had attacked... I ran out of words.

Which turned out to be just as well. Because I couldn't have got things more wrong, and walking towards us, flanked by two grinning constables, was my aunt.

27

IF YOU GO DOWN TO THE WOODS TODAY

"You all right?" Uncle Toby asked, as he touched one finger to her cheek, which had a nasty, bramble scratch slanting across it.

Aunt Madge smiled, and squeezed his hand. It occurred to me, watching that quiet, privately intimate exchange between them, how much they adored each other, and I hoped that one day I would have the privilege of sharing the same mutual respect and happiness with a husband of my own. With Laurie? It was far too soon to assume that.

Then Aunt Madge saw me. "Jan! What are you doing here? My goodness, has the world and his wife turned out just because a numbskull thought he could scare me?"

"The world, his wife and the rest of the family down to cousins four times removed," I answered with a relieved laugh. "Seriously? Are you all right?"

"Of course, I am. *He* isn't, though." She turned around and pointed to a handcuffed man who was being frog-marched between two burly, gruff-faced policemen, a growling police dog on a lead following behind. The man was wearing a long rain coat, and I guessed, by his bare legs that there was nothing underneath. One of the officers holding the man firmly by the arm had a torn mickey-mouse mask in his other hand, and I recognised the hair and coat as belonging to the same man who had startled us the other day. Except, this time, he was covered in mud, limping badly and had a thin, livid, bleeding cut across his cheek slashed from eye to jaw.

It must have hurt, (good) but I was horrified to see the tattoo on the man's neck as he turned away. It wasn't a swallow, it wasn't even a bird. The thing was a cannon. A football team insignia, he was a football fan. Eddie, I knew, sported a swallow in flight. I had been wrong. I had accused the wrong man. I felt awful.

Aunt Madge, however, misinterpreted my expression, for she patted my hand and explained, to those of us gathered round, what had happened.

"After I'd come off and the horses had bolted, he tried to grab hold of me. I was so damned cross, I kneed him in his personal bits and swiped him across the face with my riding whip."

She brandished the makeshift weapon, which was three feet long, thin, pliable and vicious if used wrongly – or rightly in this case. My aunt never used it on the horses, she carried it to remonstrate with drivers who came too close along the road. A sharp, 'thwack' on the car roof could sound very loud to those riding inside. The driver would usually stop, convinced that something had hit and damaged his paintwork – and would receive an indignant lecture from Aunt Madge pertaining to dangerous driving on the public highway. On occasion, she played her trump card when drivers threatened to report her to the police. They changed their minds when she casually informed them who she was married to.

To use her schooling whip on a man's face, however... Ouch! That would be sore for some while.

Aunt Madge folded her arms and stared at the wretched apology of a person straight in the eyes. "I then hit him over the head with a hefty stone, and knocked him out. Which enabled me to prop him up against a tree, and using the string that I always have in my pocket in case of emergency, I tied his hands behind his back on the other side of the trunk. Not wanting to leave him in case he got away, I sat down on the grass and waited for someone to come along so that I could summon assistance." She laughed, "I was expecting another rider, or a walker – not the entire district constabulary to turn up!"

We all chuckled, except for the arrested man whose scowl deepened into angry fury.

"I'll 'ave that bitch up fer assault!" he snarled.

"I wouldn't, if I were you," stated one of the policemen clutching his arm. "'Er 'usband's the DCI an' 'e don't take kindly to perverted squits like you attackin' 'is wife."

Undeterred the obnoxious man continued complaining. "I'll need stitches. I'll have a bloody scar!"

"What you'll 'ave," the constable retorted, "is yer own cell for a few years!"

Aunt Madge had heard, she stared, stern, at the man and said, "If I receive a large veterinarian bill because of you, I will know where to send it, won't I?"

She turned away then, and politely asked for someone to give her a lift to the stable yard. I went with her in one of the Panda cars. I could tell, despite the air of bravado, that she was, in fact, extremely shaken, had probably not told us everything, and was very worried about the injury to her horse. Cut knees, if deep enough, could leave scars for life, and a horse lame for a long time.

28

INTERLUDE: DC LAURIE WALKER

I didn't want to, but I had to leave Jan attending the injured horse with her aunt and the vet. I didn't know much about horses. Until I left home for college, and then university, I had ridden regularly as one of Mum and Dad's neighbours ran a working farm with sheep, cattle and a few Exmoor ponies, and I had spent many happy hours with one or other of the ponies exploring the Devon countryside. Knowing how to ride an intelligent, sturdy pony with a mind of its own, however, was completely different to helping with a distressed, sixteen-hands thoroughbred with badly damaged knees.

I had briefly explained to Jan, as tactfully as I could, that she had managed to make a mountain out of a molehill. Eddie Jones *was* a low down scumbag, to that I agreed, but he was no potential rapist. Jan had, indeed, seen his distinctive van parked outside that house on the edge of the forest on several occasions, but he was not roaming the woods seeking perverted self-gratification. *That* was taking place by romping in the bedroom with the bored, middle-aged housewife who was cheating on her frequently absent husband. Which also meant that Eddie was cheating on Gloria who worked with Jan. Given that adultery and two-timing were not criminal offences, the deceit was not our concern, and the sticky situation between Eddie and Gloria was their business to sort out, not ours.

I did try to make light of the error with Jan by cracking a joke about the tattoo. "Unfortunately, it is not a criminal offence to support a football team that has a gun carriage as a logo. The Gunners are as popular as Spurs, you know."

Jan had pulled a face. The DCI was a devout Tottenham Hotspur fan, with the two teams uncompromising rivals. Bless her, she attempted a smile, and stated, "As a yokel from the West Country, what do you know of the differences between North London football teams?"

She had a point, although I didn't add that I knew nothing about *any* football teams beyond a few famous names like Bobby Moore and Georgie Best.

I disagreed with her when she added that she had made a mess of things and would make a hopeless policewoman. In my opinion, she was astute and clever. I told her that, even if she was not cut out to be in the police, she was a super writer – I could never bash out all the words she wrote – even doing a report was hard work! She had shown me a couple of the chapters she'd written about Radger Knight. I thought the story was brilliant. But then, I thought *she* was brilliant, so I suppose there was a large element of bias involved.

As I said, I was reluctant to leave Jan, but ensuring that his wife was, indeed, unharmed, and after personally thanking every officer for their assistance, DCI Christopher directed me to the Jaguar and the road to Cambridge to continue with our previously planned visit. It would be a drive of about two hours through Saturday traffic on the main 'A' road, but we had pressing business concerning the vicious murder of an elderly lady that demanded our attention above our personal concerns, and an injured horse.

29

A CONFRONTATION

Reassuring me that she was all right, that Kaler's poor knees would heal, but he would probably have scars for the rest of his life, I left Aunt Madge at the stable yard, with a promise from her that she would get herself home as soon as possible and *rest*. I knew her promises – promises for other people *never* got broken, but for herself they lasted as long as a summer morning mist when the sun rose. About five minutes.

I cadged a lift from one of the other horse owners to the bus terminus in North Chingford, and arrived back at work just before the end of the lunch period. It did cross my mind to plead a headache and bunk off, but I knew I would only be bored at home, and sit there worrying about Laurie driving up to Cambridge for this arranged visit with Cambridgeshire Police. Which was utterly silly as Cambridge was hardly Outer Mongolia or a place rife with cutthroat murderers!

I regretted my decision about the headache a short while later. Gloria usually went to Eddie's for her lunch; she was late back, as she always was, but today she was *very* late. Mr Hurst would have had a fit had he been here. Quarter past two. Twenty past. Twenty-five past. Still no Gloria.

We had queues on the 'books in' and 'books out' sides of

the counter. I looked up from checking in someone's pile of romance novels to see Gloria storming up the front steps and thundering through the front door as if the place was on fire. My first thought was that she was hurrying because she was late, but Eddie was in hot pursuit. And the words they were shouting put paid to any theory about Gloria's tardiness.

I won't repeat what she yelled at me in front of about thirty earwigging borrowers and my colleagues, as it was most unpleasant. The gist of it being, how dare I accuse her Eddie of 'doing such disgusting things' in the forest.

I tried to explain that I had made a huge error, that I'd jumped to a wrong conclusion because of the hair colour and tattoo, but she wouldn't let me get a word in edgewise.

Eddie was avoiding making eye contact with me, and was attempting to pull Gloria away. "Leave it, girl, we all know the cops 'ave it in fer me. They tried to pin it on me, but couldn't because it weren't me. I wish I 'adn't told yer 'bout it now!"

Gloria wasn't listening to him either, she just continued shouting, and then something clicked inside me. Normally, where unpleasant confrontations were concerned, I would have wanted the ground to swallow me up, even if whatever it was had not been my fault. But it had been a trying, emotional week. I stood behind the relatively safe barricade of the library counter, fists on hips, absolutely *furious*. Which is a shame, as maybe I should not have said what I then said: "It's what your Eddie was doing in a fifty-something's *bedroom* that you ought to be concerned about, Gloria!"

I've often wondered about the phrase 'all hell broke loose'. It was quite spectacular to see it in action. Accusations were traded with vehement denials backwards and forwards between the two of them, with Eddie challenging Gloria about where *she* had been last Saturday night – and who with. "That damned Joe 'Arper down the road, I bet! You've been makin' eyes at 'im these last bloody weeks, ain't yer?"

Gloria's returned salvo was of a similar damning nature.

"Why wouldn't I go out with him? He treats me proper. He doesn't knock me about like you do, you toad!"

And then she turned on me, her eyes narrowed, full of venom. "As for you, you little hoity-toity madam, stay out of my business. In fact, stay out of my life, I never want to see you again."

Thankfully, Pamela emerged from the office, announced that the police had been called and demanded that the pair of them vacate the library immediately. Which, to my surprise, but relief, they did, although the state of play was only removed from inside the library to outside, where the row continued with increased shouting and shoving.

I felt awful. Gloria had been my friend, or so I thought. I should never have said what I said, but it had slipped out. How could I have been so stupid?

Our intrigued borrowers, meanwhile, hurried to the windows to watch the proceedings.

A Panda car turned up quite quickly – on patrol in the area – with two young constables who handcuffed and arrested Eddie and Gloria on a charge of public affray. I did wonder whether it was wise to transport them to the police station in the same vehicle, but that was the constables' problem.

It all seemed very quiet once they had gone.

"She'll get the sack for this," Trish assured me. "It's not the first time she's caused a scene."

One of our borrowers, a lovely lady, Mrs Delbourne, summed everything up rather nicely, I thought.

"Better than them police programmes that are on the telly, that were!" she declared with a hearty laugh.

30

A GRIM TALE

Uncle Toby arrived home that Saturday evening quite late. Aunt Madge and I ate together, and we left the rest of the delicious slow-cooked beef casserole in the lower oven of the Aga for Uncle Toby and Laurie, then she had taken herself off for a hot, relaxing bath, and bed. The events of the day had caught up with her, but at least Kaler's injuries had proven to not be as serious as we had first thought; the poor boy was stiff and sore, however, and would be off work for some weeks. I suspected that my aunt was also stiff, sore and bruised, but she would never let on. Although, I did glimpse her swallowing down a couple of Panadol tablets, rather naughtily along with a dram of whisky. I pretended that I hadn't noticed.

I dished up a generous helping of beef, dumplings and vegetables for my uncle and Laurie when they eventually arrived home, and, not bothering to use the dining room, we sat together at the kitchen table. While they ate, they told me all that they had discovered. It turned out to be a grim tale.

"We had to liaise with Cambridgeshire police," Laurie explained between mouthfuls of steaming hot chunks of prime beef. "What we hadn't realised, after speaking to the garrulous Mrs Munday in Appletree Road – she was very different from her unhelpful husband, although just as condescending – was that Mrs Norris's daughter, Irene, had recently died under suspicious circumstances."

I stared at him unbelieving. "What?" I eventually managed to ask.

"Irene's grandson had been taken from his pram," Uncle Toby said.

My eyes widened at his additional comment. "Not the baby who was found dead the other day? How awful!"

My uncle nodded. "Mmm hmmm. Awful indeed. There seems to be a connection between the murder of Mrs Norris and that of her daughter, Irene. And the baby."

"And," Laurie added, after blowing on a hot chunk of potato to cool it a little, "Mrs Norris's granddaughter, the baby's aunt, Susan Dunster, is missing."

He fetched out a crumpled black and white photograph from his pocket and showed it to me. It was an image of an old coach-built pram. I stared at it, open mouthed, looked up, gaped at Laurie, then at my uncle. Back at the photograph.

"But, but," I stammered, "this is the pram we saw. The one that woman was pushing. It had a squeaky wheel. The woman who said she was going to buy powdered milk." I pointed to a deep scratch along the side. I'd forgotten all about it, but seeing it again now, I clearly recalled it.

"I remember thinking that this scratch looked like a shepherd's crook." I pointed to the hook shape at the start of the long, white mark that swept along the body of the pram.

"Going to buy powdered milk from a shop that closed at ten-thirty?" Laurie said, as he handed me a second photograph of a plastic handbag. I studied it carefully.

"It *looks* identical to the one Mrs Norris had. Where was it found?" I spoke in a whisper, barely daring to want to hear the answer.

"In the pram with the dead baby."

"The pram," my uncle interrupted, "which was stolen from Lloyd's Park in Walthamstow. The owner was using the ladies' lavatories to change her baby's nappy. Came out, no pram. A minor Walthamstow incident that no one had any reason to connect to the more serious missing Cambridgeshire boy until this afternoon. When we turned up, and two-and-two was duly added to make a very firm four."

"But," I frowned, confused, "the baby in that pram, the one our woman was pushing, was a girl, not a boy."

"Was it?" Uncle asked quietly.

I considered. He was right, I had assumed a girl because the woman had said 'she'.

Laurie produced a third photograph, as if he were a magician pulling rabbits from a top hat. "Recognise her?"

My hand flew to my mouth. "Oh, my goodness. It's her, yes, the woman who had been pushing the pram."

Uncle Toby mopped gravy with a chunk of buttered bread. "Susan Dunster, Mrs Norris's youngest granddaughter."

Laurie laid his hand on mine, gave a gentle squeeze. "The baby in the pram that night was already dead, Jan. That's why there was no sound of crying. Naturally, we simply thought that the child was asleep, but the poor little mite had died several hours earlier, before or after Mrs Norris had been killed, we do not know. Unless we find Mrs Dunster and get a confession, we may never know. The nappy had been left soiled and unchanged for at least a day, that was the smell."

"And I suppose it was she who dumped those other soiled nappies in that man's dustbin?"

Both Laurie and my uncle frowned, puzzled. I explained about Mr Jones who had been vociferously complaining to Sergeant Tanner.

"We didn't know about that," Laurie admitted.

"Why would you?" I pointed out. "There was no reason for the desk sergeant to connect the two... As we didn't connect the woman with the pram and Mrs Norris."

My uncle filled in the rest of what they thought they knew, speaking matter-of-factly. "We can't be sure, but if the jigsaw pieces fit together, as we and the Cambridgeshire police believe they will, it's likely that Susan Dunster pushed her mother down the stairs – the injuries are not quite concurrent with a mere fall – and then took the baby."

"But why?" I asked, aware that I was uttering far too many 'buts'.

"The how first, hmm?" Uncle Toby said with a slight, indulgent smile. "We now know that she caught a train from Cambridge to London's Liverpool Street, then another to Walthamstow, presumably carrying the child. From Walthamstow, to get to Chingford on foot, she would have cut through Lloyd's Park. It's quicker and shorter. We assume she saw the pram, stole it, then walked on to her grandmother's house. Her fingerprints, found at her mother's house in Cambridgeshire, and all over the pram, match those we found at Mrs Norris's." He paused a moment, gathering his thoughts. Considering the right thing to say? "The same fingerprints were found on the broken frame of the mirror."

She, Susan Dunster, must have used some force, I thought as I got up to put the kettle on to make coffee, and then fetched raspberry tart and cream from the refrigerator. It had not been a large mirror, but a heavy one with its wooden frame and backboard. Given the right force, it would have done a lot of damage. *Did* do a lot of damage.

Coffee poured and tart served, Laurie continued with the sorry tale of fact and pieced together assumptions. "It is possible that Mrs Norris may have assumed that the child was Susan's own baby. There was no reason for her not to. She had no telephone; from what we have discovered she'd had very little contact with her family for several years. There had been a falling out between them because of her gambling on the greyhounds."

"But why assume the baby was Susan's?" There, another 'but'.

"Cecily had sent her grandmother a birthday card."

I drew a breath, interrupted Laurie with, "It was on the mantlepiece in the front room."

He nodded. "It was."

I added hastily, "I didn't touch it, of course, so I had no idea who it was from."

"Cecily had sent it; there was a scribbled note on the inside, although we didn't realise its significance until talking with Cambridgeshire police and Cecily herself. The note was a quick mention that she'd given birth to another son, and that Susan also had a new baby, but Cecily hadn't said whether it was a boy or girl."

"So, Mrs Norris must have assumed the baby was Susan's?" I said.

My uncle took up the sorry tale. "Cambridgeshire CID have discovered from Cecily and her husband – the parents of the missing boy, that is – that Susan had given birth to a daughter, but the child died at six-weeks old. Susan had previously suffered several miscarriages, and her firstborn had also passed away at two months. It is possible that, in her considerable mental strain, she thought that her sister's baby was her own." Sadness tinged his voice. "Mothers will do strange things when there are tragic circumstances."

We were all silent a moment. I noticed my uncle patting his pockets, a habit he had when stressed, unconsciously searching for the pipe and tobacco that he no longer smoked.

"Mrs Norris might have started having suspicions, something else we will never know, but it is likely that when she saw the newspaper on the Friday, about the missing boy, she realised the truth. The article gave Irene Batewell's name, and that of Cecily's."

Tears were brimming in my eyes. "Poor Mrs Norris! What a shock it all must have been for her – no wonder she left the library in such a hurry!" I was appalled. That poor old lady! The boy's poor parents!

I couldn't find it in my heart to feel sorry for Susan.

I wondered aloud: "Did Mrs Norris draw out the money

she had saved from her winnings at the dog track to give to her granddaughter? Maybe it wasn't enough, or they argued, or Mrs Norris confronted her about the child or..."

"...Or, for whatever reason, Susan lost her temper, hit her gran over the head with the first thing that had come to hand – that heavy, wooden-framed mirror hanging on the kitchen wall," Laurie finished for me.

"Cambridgeshire think it likely," Uncle said, leaning back in his chair, "that she might have killed her other babies. There is going to be further investigation into how they died."

"Could that happen?" I blurted out naïvely. "Would a mother deliberately kill her own child?"

Uncle Toby's face was unreadable. Very quietly he said, "It has happened before, Jan. It has happened before."

The telephone rang, the sound shrill in the silence. Wiping his mouth with a napkin, Uncle Toby looked briefly at the kitchen clock – it was well past eleven – and went to answer it. Laurie and I listened intently, catching only a few words: "I see." "Yes." "I understand."

While he was talking, Aunt Madge came down in her dressing gown, apologising to Laurie for not being dressed, her hair a mess and no make-up.

"You look quite lovely as you are," he said gallantly as he pulled a chair out for her, asked if she wanted anything.

"A cup of tea would go down well," she answered with a tired smile. "I was asleep, the phone woke me. Have I missed anything?"

I filled her in while Laurie made the tea. I'm not sure if he heard her whisper, when he was fetching milk from the fridge, "Mark my words. He's a keeper, this one, Jan!"

Didn't I know it!

Uncle Toby came back into the kitchen, his face a mask of weariness. He'd been on the phone quite a while. "I could do with a large whisky," he said absent-mindedly kissing the top of Aunt Madge's head. "My dear? Laurie?"

Laurie nodded, but Aunt Madge indicated her tea. I

fetched the two men a generous tot. For myself, I had a gin and tonic. Well, tonic with a splash of gin. I don't like it too strong.

Uncle took Aunt Madge's hand in his, idly stroking the wedding ring on her finger with his thumb, waiting until I had sat down at the table again.

"That was Cambridgeshire. Susan Dunster was arrested two hours ago. She was caught trying to remove a baby from a pram while the mother was in a shop. Quick thinking from the shop owner who realised what was happening."

"Do they know where she's been all this while?" Laurie asked, after taking a sip of his drink.

"Living rough, they think. Sleeping out under the elm trees along The Backs behind King's College."

"Oh, poor girl, she must be in such a turmoil," Aunt Madge said with genuine sympathy.

I couldn't echo it. "Poor mother," I snorted. "The thought of what might have happened to her baby will stay with her for a long while!"

Uncle Toby looked grim and sad all in one. He took a deep breath. "I agree with you, Jan. I cannot feel sorry for Susan. The baby boy, his name was Billy, by the way, had been killed with one of those dangly woollen pom-pom toys. The ball had been stuffed into his mouth, to keep him quiet, presumably. He choked. Suffocated. But to make sure he was dead she had wound the toy's cord around his little neck and pulled it tight."

I bit my lip to stem the flow of tears. Laurie noticed, took my hand in his.

"What will become of her?" Aunt Madge asked.

Her husband shrugged. "Prison for a long time, I expect, if found guilty. Unlikely that she'll not be, there's a stack of evidence against her. Psychiatric mental institution, perhaps?"

We were all silent a moment, mulling over our own thoughts.

"I usually enjoy policework," Laurie said with a slight sigh, "but these sort of things..." He didn't finish the sentence, a shrug filling in the missing words.

"There are a lot of things we'd rather not see, or do, son," Uncle Toby said. "I concentrate on the results, the achievements, not the failures, or the vile acts of some of our fellow human beings. You need a tough stomach and an open mind to get through some of what we have to face, but what would the world be if we weren't here to do what we do? Try to do."

"You're a good copper, Laurie," Aunt Madge stated, reaching across the table to pat his arm. "And we need good coppers. Coppers who notice enough to care."

Laurie still had my hand in his, he rubbed his thumb over my knuckles. "Thank you, Jan – thank you, Mrs Christopher; sir. I'm just tired. Being a little self-indulgent maudlin, perhaps. It's been a long day." He smiled, said, more positively, "I'll be taking my Detective Sergeant's exams soon." A little sheepishly, added, "And maybe, one day, my Inspector's?"

Uncle Toby gave a soft chuckle. "Good luck with that, then."

I made a mental note to ensure that Laurie realised what my uncle had meant: that he had earned his respect and approval. I knew Laurie was worrying about being transferred back to Hackney, a place, and colleagues, he did not much like. I hoped that, maybe, with Uncle's influence, there would be a permanent position for him at Chingford.

"These sort of events, senseless murder for instance," Laurie continued, "are hard to come to terms with, especially where an innocent child is concerned. To finish a case in your mind, file it away as 'job done' is not easy to do." He paused, had a gulp of the whisky. "I suppose it doesn't really matter, but the second woollen ball that would have been on the other end of that cord is still missing. I don't know why, that small bit of extra proof, perhaps? But I wish we'd found it."

"We can't always tie up the loose ends," Uncle Toby said, then laughed sardonically at his unintentional pun. Gallows humour to lighten a dark subject. "A loose end, literally, in this case. It'll turn up, I expect."

I looked from one to the other, uncertain whether to say anything.

Aunt Madge noticed my hesitation and raised an eyebrow, questioningly.

"Didn't SOCO find it?" I queried. "I saw a blue, woolly ball under the little table in Mrs Norris's front room. I thought it was a cat's toy."

So sad that a toy, meant to bring pleasure to a little life, had so cruelly ended it.

"We'll have to check the evidence boxes again," my uncle said, then, picking up his glass, leant forward to chink it against Laurie's. "Live for today, son, and have faith in tomorrow. The world isn't all bad, there are *some* good things to cherish."

He smiled at his young Detective Constable, and cast a surreptitious wink towards me.

END WORD

A lot has happened in the years since 1971, not so much 'water under the bridge', more like a full spate flood at times. A good bit of it was fun; some of it wasn't.

As I sit here, gazing out of the window during this time of enforced lockdown, I'm aware that my agent will do her pieces when she discovers that I have digressed into writing this, the first of an intended series, loosely based on a boxful of old diaries which I found when rummaging in the attic.

I'll tell her that old ladies get whims, and it's best to indulge us. You can get away with things when you shuffle past your mid-sixties, especially if people think you're an eccentric old biddy.

I encourage the thought. It's far more entertaining.

What's that saying? *"Rather than spend a dreary, sensible life, I'd prefer to skid into my grave with a chocolate bar in one hand, a bottle of Champagne in the other, shouting, 'whoo-hoo that was fun!'."*

I heard on the BBC Radio news, a few weeks ago, that Susan Dunster, had passed away in her sleep at the secure mental prison where she had spent her days since 1971. Even after all these years, I don't feel sorry for her.

I did see Gloria again on a crowded underground train in London, but she either did not see me, or deliberately ignored me. I suspect the latter. It hurt, at the time, the thought that someone could despise me so much, but I don't mind what people think of me now. It gradually dawned on me that they don't care what *I* think or do, so why get upset about them?

Ah, I'm being called for lunch. The dogs have just come in from a walk. I hope there are no muddy paws. It was raining earlier, although the sun is coming out, sparkling on the grass as if fairies have scattered thousands of tiny diamonds all around.

Quite beautiful.

I've never forgotten what my dear Uncle Toby said that evening. *"Live for today and have faith in tomorrow. The world isn't all bad, there are some good things to cherish."*

How right he was.

Until next time,

Jan

AUTHOR'S NOTE

This is a work of fiction, but for those interested in factual detail: South Chingford Branch Library was a real library. The building is still there in Hall Lane, but it is no longer a library. I worked there from 1969 when I left Wellington Avenue Secondary School for Girls at the age of sixteen, until 1982.

Apart from the murder, many of the library 'anecdotes' used in this tale really happened – an elderly lady did come in every day to cut out the coupons from the newspapers, and yes, a young lad did ask for a book about copper knickers. I was, also, threatened with the sack by a head librarian (of a different library) because of reading a newspaper. Unfortunately, I had no DC Walker to rescue me, and I was too lacking in self-confidence to defend myself back then.

Now, as a sixty-seven-year-old (at the time of writing this) I would have given that odious man a piece of my mind about his unacceptable bullying.

This real librarian, I must add, was *not* a Mr Hurst and did not (as far as I know!) have my fictional character's personal 'interests', but I do confess, I thoroughly enjoyed inventing the character and getting my own back in a roundabout sort of way!

Many of the street names and places also exist – except for those where 'police incidents' (such as a murder!) happened, the exception being Epping Forest where I did encounter 'flashers' on several occasions while out riding in the 1970s. Fortunately, however, I was never involved in anything more serious. Rajah and Kaler, by the way, were two of the horses I have had the pleasure to own in the past.

One additional note, the episode of the green Morris Minor car sliding down the hill with me in it, is all true. The only difference, it was my dad who rescued me, not a fictitious Uncle Toby, and it might have been a plastic toy telescope that I was playing with, not a recorder.

As much as possible I have checked and researched the little details to ensure they are accurate. I have changed one or two minor things for the convenience of the story: the film (almost no one in England called them 'movies back in the '60s and '70s) *Kelly's Heroes* was released in 1970, and probably did not have a repeat showing at the 'pictures' in 1971, but usually not a fan of war movies I couldn't resist using this one as it is one of my favourites, and it set me back an entire afternoon while writing this story, as it was on the TV – again! Hopefully, the 'positive waves' emitted by Oddball (Donald Sutherland) has brought me some good vibes!

The *Jackie* magazine is accurate regarding the cover and content, but the real magazine (issue no: 395) came out on Saturday 31st July, not on the Thursday. One 'fact' I have not been able to verify is when the bridle paths, designated as horse rides, were re-surfaced from natural earth tracks to all weather, supposedly well-drained (hah!) tracks. I remember the vehicles doing the work, but not *when*. My apologies for the error if this work was undertaken after 1971.

I have a few very special people to thank for their help and support:

Authors: Mysteries/crime - Debbie Young, Susan Grossey, Lucienne Boyce, Jane Harlond. Alternative (and a new mystery series) - Alison Morton. Historical fiction - Annie Whitehead, Anna Belfrage, Elizabeth St. John. Short stories and contemporary Richard Tearle. Children's - Caz Greenham. I highly recommend them all as excellent novelists.

A huge thank you to those who read early drafts and gave me enormously appreciated feedback: graphics designer, Cathy Helms; Lynne Harmon, Nicky Galliers, Richard Ashen of South Chingford Community Library and again to Alison Morton who kindly supervised the formatting.

Most sincerely meant - *thank you* to all of you – my readers. Can I ask? If you have the time, please do leave a few words on Amazon for me. You never know, I might use your kind comment in my next novel!

http://viewauthor.at/HelenHollick

Finally, I began writing this tale during the initial UK lockdown of the Covid-19 pandemic. Perhaps it's good to know that *some* positive things came out of those unprecedented, un-normal, often frustrating spring months of 2020.

ABOUT HELEN HOLLICK

After an exciting Lottery win on the opening night of the 2012 London Olympic Games, Helen moved from a North-East London suburb to an eighteenth-century farmhouse in North Devon, where she lives with her husband, daughter and son-in-law, and a variety of pets and animals, which include three moorland-bred Exmoor ponies.

Her study overlooks part of the Taw Valley, where the main road runs from Exeter to Barnstaple, and back in the 1600s troops of the English Civil Wars marched to and from battle. There are several friendly ghosts sharing the house and farm, and Helen regards herself as merely a temporary custodian of the lovely old house, not its owner.

First published in 1994 with her Arthurian *Pendragon's Banner Trilogy*, her passion is her pirate character, Captain Jesamiah Acorne of the nautical adventure series *The Sea Witch Voyages*, which have been snapped up by US-based, independent publisher Penmore Press.

Helen became a USA Today Bestseller with her historical novel *The Forever Queen* (titled *A Hollow Crown* in the UK), the story of Anglo-Saxon Queen Emma of Normandy, which is a prequel to *Harold The King* (titled *I Am The Chosen King* in the

US) and is the story of events that led to the 1066 Battle of Hastings.

Recognised by her stylish hats, Helen attends conferences and book-related events when she can, as a chance to meet her readers and social-media followers, although her "wonky eyesight", as she describes her condition of Glaucoma, is becoming a little prohibitive for travel. She founded and runs the Discovering Diamonds review blog for historical fiction, and is a regular blogger, Facebooker and Tweeter.

She occasionally gets time to write...

Website: www.helenhollick.net
Newsletter: http://tinyletter.com/HelenHollick
Twitter: @HelenHollick
Email author@helenhollick.net

COMING SOON...

A MYSTERY OF MURDER
A Jan Christopher Mystery Book 2
By Helen Hollick

Wednesday, 22nd December 1971
When Doubts Arise...

The thought of driving all the way from London to Devon with my boyfriend, Laurie, for Christmas was exciting, but tinged with a smattering of reluctance. It would mean leaving my beloved legal guardians, my Uncle Toby and Aunt Madge, behind.

I'd not had a Christmas or a New Year without them since they'd adopted me when I was orphaned at five years old. At almost nineteen, independence was knocking at the door, but all the same, I was concerned about leaving them for the duration of the festivities. Concerns which Aunt Madge soon put an end to.

"Goodness, Jan, we've been looking forward to a Christmas on our own for the past, I don't know how many years!"

I wasn't sure if she was being serious or joking. Her grin gave the game away. Joke.

They had taken me under their wing after my father had been shot dead, and my mother... well, she died soon after, but we never talked about it. All I know is that she had been under severe mental strain from when my identical twin, June, died after an illness.

I still resented June because she was the second born, and got the name 'June' for the month we were conceived. I got the name of the month we were prematurely born; January. Fortunately, everyone called me Jan. It could have been worse: February as a name would have been ghastly!

Uncle Toby was my dad's brother, and his response to my worries about Christmas was a little less blunt, bless him. "We can't all be off on merry jaunts at the same time, Jan. The crime rate would soar, and Chingford Police wouldn't cope!"

My uncle, in his working capacity, was DCI Tobias Christopher. Laurie – Lawrence Walker – had recently been promoted to Detective Sergeant. Important people within the realm of law enforcement, although I suspected the North London suburb of Chingford would survive without them both for ten days. There were, after all, *other* men (and a few women) in CID.

For myself I was quite happy to take ten days off from working as an assistant in our local library. It was always busy in the run-up to the holiday closing, and while I would miss out on the boxes of chocolates and tins of buttery shortbread, given to the staff by appreciative members of the public, my already too broad waistline would not suffer from it.

My main fear, however, was meeting Laurie's parents. I had spoken to them on the telephone several times and they seemed nice, but I had been going out with Laurie since late July, would they assume that our relationship was becoming serious?

Come to that, did *I* assume it was serious? By accepting

the invitation, was I committing myself to a possible life as a policeman's wife? Or was I reading too much into things? I mean, spending Christmas with your boyfriend's family didn't mean a marriage proposal, did it? Or did it? Then there was the question, did I, or didn't I, *want* it to mean just that?

Had I known what was to happen soon after we had arrived at Mr and Mrs Walker's lovely old West Country house, my apprehensions would have dwindled to nothing.

Discovering the grisly evidence of what was clearly murder – the buried remains of two decapitated heads – followed by unpleasant suspicions, and sordid accusations, were to ruin Christmas, and stretch loyalties to the limit...

PRAISE FOR HELEN HOLLICK'S NOVELS

"Helen Hollick has it all! She tells a great story, gets her history right, and writes consistently readable books" – Bernard Cornwell

"A novel of enormous emotional power" – Elizabeth Chadwick

"In the sexiest pirate contest, Cpt Jesamiah Acorne gives Jack Sparrow a run for his money!" – Sharon K. Penman

"Thanks to Hollick's masterful storytelling Harold's nobility and heroism enthral to the point of engendering hope for a different ending to the famous battle of 1066" – Publisher's Weekly

"If only all historical fiction could be this good" – Historical Novel Association Reviews

"Most impressive" – The Lady

"Helen Hollick's series about piratical hero Jesamiah Acorne and his mystical wife Tiola Oldstagh provides a real comfort read that seamlessly blends history, fantasy, and romance with plenty of action and suspense while also further developing the characters with every new book." – Amazon reviewer

ALSO BY HELEN HOLLICK

The Pendragon's Banner Trilogy
The Kingmaking: Book One
Pendragon's Banner: Book Two
Shadow of the King: Book Three

The Saxon 1066 Series
A Hollow Crown (UK edition title)
The Forever Queen (US edition title. USA Today bestseller)
Harold the King (UK edition title)
I Am The Chosen King (US edition title)

1066 Turned Upside Down (alternative short stories by
various authors)

**The Sea Witch Voyages of the pirate,
Captain Jesamiah Acorne**

Sea Witch: The first voyage
Pirate Code: The second voyage
Bring It Close: The third voyage
Ripples In The Sand: The fourth voyage
On The Account: The fifth voyage
To Follow
Gallows Wake: The sixth voyage
When The Mermaid Sings: *a novella prequel.*

———

Betrayal
Short stories by various authors

NON-FICTION
Pirates: Truth and Tales
Life Of A Smuggler: In Fact And Fiction

Discovering The Diamond (with Jo Field)

———

BEFORE YOU GO....
I hope you've enjoyed the first of Jan's adventures , and I
wonder if I could ask you something...
Would you leave a review on Amazon? It really does help to
spread the word and bring new readers in to discover Jan's
world.
Here's the link:
http://viewauthor.at/HelenHollick

Thank you!

**And if you have a moment, here's how to thank your
favourite authors:**
'Like' and 'follow' where you can on social media
Subscribe to their newsletter
Buy a copy of your favourite book as a present to give
pleasure to others

Printed in Great Britain
by Amazon